# NAKED CHRONICLES OF A GAY MAN

Volume

*"Boredom and Dullness are the biggest diseases in the world."*

*Freddie Mercury*

*"Most of us in the gay world deal with some form of deep-seated shame. Considering we grow up in a predominantly 'straight man's world', where inevitably we feel 'less than' — It is perhaps no surprise. I believe that in order to navigate through this, there has to be some ownership of it. Laying our ashamedness bare... so to speak, and then acknowledging it. On some level accepting it, on some level admonishing it, and on some level finding our healing in it."*

*Marcus Olozulu*

*This book is fiction and is for adults only.*
*If you're easily offended then please put the book down now.*
*You've been warned.*

# Acknowledgements

This book would not have been possible without the openness of all those interviewed during my research. Most accounts are fiction, and names of characters were of course changed in the material that wasn't. There has been distortion created in all areas of this project for literary purposes. Nonetheless, the research was validated to the best of my ability, through a lot of questioning. My curiosity for another human being has never been so ignited as it was during this project.

I also have to express my sincere gratitude to a writer whose work I greatly admire. She offered her much restricted time to proofread this book. Thank you. You know who you are. ;)

I'm very excited about finally being able to share this. It's been a project that has added to my personal growth in a very big way. Writing this book has 'hammered' down on the judgement aspect of my personality...a lot, whilst leaving room for empathy. My hope and wish is that it does the same for the reader.

I should say that the book is written for adults' consumption only. It is purposely crude and very raw with a lot of sexual content. So if you are easily offended, then please put the book down now.

## TRYING TOO HARD

So, I finally get a good kick up the arse in the department of — 'Do not force things to happen!'

Desperation has slowly taken a hold of me. I am now the epitome of 'desperare' — The latin derivative for desperation. I am most certainly losing hope and entrenched in despair over being single. I'm turning 50 you see, surely it's time to settle down with someone. No good will come out of waiting patiently for the one to just walk into my life mysteriously. I need to get out of the habit of random hookups. Need to be able to sit with my loneliness, just long enough to come out the other side, where hopefully there will be acceptance and a fearless sense of peace.

There's no time, I tell myself continuously. I'm getting older. Don't take my youthful looks for granted — sooner or later, age will manifest itself in wrinkles, haggardness, sparkle-diminished eyes, aches and creaks, lethargy, leaky guts and orifices; etcetera. Luck will run out — How hard can it be to find someone? Surely it should be easier. Join better apps, reduce my standards — maybe a little. I tell myself I'm special and so deserve someone special, but c'mon now. If a guy aged 27 to 35 wants to be with you, that can't be bad right. It says something, must be youthful and certainly must have something going for me. I mean, 15 to 23 years difference, definitely must mean something? Or does it? All trying too hard? Desperation?

After a couple of ghosting episodes, I meet a guy on the back of someone else that I picked up, metaphorically speaking. I didn't actually have one guy clinging on to the back of another guy — I'll explain. The first was drugged to the eyeballs and wanted fucking. As should...Pardon? — Oh, what is ghosting? It's a 'thing,' now where someone you've been chatting to for weeks, sometimes months, suddenly stops communicating with you. Disappears off the ether, hence the term. Sometimes they reappear for a couple of weeks or months — only to disappear again. That's called submarining — Yup that's the dating world now.

Yeah...so as expected with the guy I pick up who is as high as a kite. He passes out...mid penetration. I tell myself it was the sheer pleasure from the girth of my cock, that made him pass out. That's what I'll always tell myself. Not willing to accept anything else. He had been up all night and done too much G. Sure, it was a contributing factor, but the pleasure from my cock was the thing that pushed him over the edge, and he literally passed out.

I cover him up with a blanket, so he can sleep — hoping he doesn't go into a coma. I go on Grindr again to see if there are any other potential shags — I have the horn now you see, must get some sex. When I'm horny, I swear it's like a curse. Sorry?... Oh, apologies — Grindr is a gay dating app. The term 'dating' is used very loosely. It might as well be called a gay shagging app.

Back to my libido — Its so bad sometimes, I've fantasized about castration before, because I feel such a slave to my sex drive. A friend once said to me that sometimes men are just so desperate to put it somewhere, anywhere, to see if something happens. To see if *anything* happens. Out of sheer boredom. I think that kind of sums it up.

Alas, my Grindr bait is taken. He's a top, just what I need. An arrogant dominating top to roger me senseless. It's what I mostly want anyway, much prefer to be fucked. So much more pleasure than doing the fucking. I use the analogy here of cleaning our ears with Q-tips. Instead of Q-tips I tend to use the long end of the cap of a bic crystal pen, so much safer when you have a knack for doing this. The visceral pleasure derived from cleaning your ear is — I would say — on the top of the list of little guilty pleasures, and all due to the sensitive nerve endings in the ear canal. I liken the ear canal to your butthole and whatever implement you use to probe your ear, I liken to the penis. Hopefully, you make sense of my analogy. Basically, the women in straight relationships I believe have most of the fun. You don't hear of men having multiple orgasms. Straight men anyway. But yes — gay men can.

This new guy seems keen, he wants to come straight over. I look at the guy who has passed out in my bed. I'm still a bit worried. What if he falls into a coma, or even worse dies. I move closer and can hear heavy breathing which eventually turns to snoring. Phew. Good. Alive. I can shut the door, pretend he's not there when the other guy comes. Thank god for my spare bedroom. Will the new guy hear the snoring and wonder? Will he ask questions? Will I have to lie to him? Easy — 'a friend of mine partied hard last night and passed out.' That's not the biggest white lie I ever told. Him being a white guy could add *some* 'out of context truth' to it. Does that even make sense?

Anyway, will the new guy hear him snore through my moaning? Hopefully not. I moan...loud, and a lot. Especially if he has girth and plays with my nipples with sexualised attention. That's my thing. My nipples are hard-wired, you see. I lose myself completely when they are being played with. Tweaked, slowly caressed, sucked, licked, gently bitten, flicked — all of those in any succession turns me on like a well oiled carburettor. I should rephrase that — All of that, guarantees my being present to the moment. Come to think of it, it's possibly the only activity that ensures I don't go into my head. Meditation does not accomplish it, gardening doesn't either. Cooking does at times — You kind of have to pay attention, otherwise you could slice your fingers. When I'm writing...Mmmm, maybe to a degree, But I still need to rummage in my head for creative threads to use in my prose, so surely this doesn't count.

The guy is on his way. I douche in preparation. I tend to do it at least three times, to be extra safe. My tummy feels okay. You have to understand your tummy. If I have the runs, it'll probably be a disaster. You just know a certain kind of tummy may be risky. Not always though, sometimes you think all is well, and then...oops 'poonami.' You most certainly need to know your own tummy. I pride myself on being somewhat aware of my stomach and whether to be worried about an accident or not. The smell when I've been wrong sometimes — oh my god! It's the worst thing! There is no getting hard after that. For anyone involved. Sex is cancelled.

This time I feel pretty confident that my insides are clean. I wash my anus one more time to ensure it's cleanliness. You know...just in case he enjoys rimming. Most dominant tops enjoy rimming and I sure do enjoy being rimmed. Not as much as I like my nipples played with, but it's a close second. I smell my finger afterwards. Midnight Plum and Wild Blackberry is all I smell. I smile. All good. I listen out for snoring and can't hear anything now. I walk back to the room he's in with some nervous energy, I open the door and I'm relieved to hear he's still snoring. Don't think I've ever been more happy to hear someone snore. He can't be dead and snore, he has to be breathing. So again, all good. I close the door gently behind me, pleased with the way things are panning out. My phone pings and vibrates. Most gay guys recognise this sound and most gay guys know intuitively it's the sound of a possible hookup. It's a welcoming excitable sound. It normally means someone might be getting some sex. It's an extra release of dopamine compared to those just getting a ping from a social media app.

I sit down on the stairway, slightly aware of a little pleasant soreness in my bum hole from douching. *When did all this become so normal?* I wonder to myself. I have a guy that I started to fuck who's just passed out in my bedroom, and I'm now waiting for another guy to fuck me in the spare room. *When did all this become okay?* I shrug my shoulders. I'm horny. It didn't work out with one guy and I have the option of another. Don't need to overthink it. My face attempts to reconfigure between a slight grimace and a smile. I remember now that the new guy on his way had typed that he likes a guy waiting for him in a jock strap. I press onto my feet and rush to my bedroom. Not long now the front doorbell will go. I slowly open the bedroom door and I'm immediately comforted by the sound of more deep snoring. I tip-toe into the room, even though I'm pretty convinced there'll be no stir from him. He looks dead to the world, lying there in a stranger's bed. Possibly one of the best sleeps he gets — Drugged to his eyeballs.

I find my only jockstrap tucked away to the side of my underwear drawer. I pick it up and back out of the room again, closing the door in slow motion behind me. Now convinced there will be no way this guy wakes up in the next few hours. I should be able to moan to my heart's content in the next room, and not worry about him waking up and walking in on us. Though that might be a turn on for all concerned, I rather that didn't happen. Complicated enough as it is. I'm already a slut. I own my sluttiness, no need to push it.

The doorbell goes just as I pull the jockstrap up. I never used to like jockstraps — because I felt it made you slutty. I laugh to myself. *'Own your sluttiness and own the jockstrap pal.'* I grab and wear a bathrobe and go down the stairs. I check that it's definitely him, by looking through the door viewer. Convinced it's him, I open the door with a neutral face. It's never the expression you have on your face when you open the door to a friend. Now I come to think of it, I always open the door to a one-off sexual encounter with a somewhat stoic face. The guy smiles a little. I believe I force a smile, not so sure. I'm not too bothered or aware of what my face is doing or portraying. I just want to get fucked. Nonetheless, I'm not completely devoid of etiquette. I ask if he wants a drink. He says some water will be good. It's often water that hookups need to drink. The nervous excitement normally dries your mouth out, you see. Kissing with a dry mouth is like chewing on a paper towel. I let the guy in and close the door gently. Not out of concern of waking the other guy up, but because that is what I do when closing the door to a guy that has walked in for sex. I close the door quietly, as if somehow a slammed door might destroy the sexual tension.

As I walk past him to get to the kitchen. I recall a situation in a sauna where a guy made it obvious he fancied me. It's very easy for men to show that they fancy someone when naked, something women can't do. I had ruined the moment by talking. I tried to make small talk. Mostly to calm my nerves. The guy looked at me as if I was an alien. I never knew there was a ritual for certain environments. Dark rooms and saunas. You don't talk. You just fuck. Speaking eliminates the tension. The tension was what added to the turn on. You talk, you missed out getting laid. I learnt quickly.

I fetch a glass and fill it with water from the tap. I turn around and hand him the filled glass. I feel confident. I only vaguely remember when I lacked confidence in these situations. I used to remember when my heart raced. Not now. Not anymore. Now there was a kind of numbness. There was some excitement but it was dulled. I would say there was probably no more excitement than finding a hot porn video to watch. He gulps his water down. He's not as physically fit as me, which makes me even more confident. He's good-looking though, he has even, white teeth. But he's a little overweight, that never did do it for me. But he's a top and he was going to take charge and that makes up for it. I utter that we go upstairs and I lead the way. As I walk into the guest bedroom I'm certain I hear snoring from the other guy in my room. I drop my robe immediately, revealing my jockstrap. Hopefully, this act will outweigh this top's capacity to listen. I turn around and we kiss. It's a sensual kiss. Not too sloppy, tender but firm. The kiss tells me he wants me and he wants me bad. This excites me. He turns me around and bends me over so he can put his tongue in my arse. I listen out for anymore snoring from the other guy and hear nothing. I relax into the pleasure being received by my hook up's mouth.

He asks for a condom. I hate condoms, but I find him one. He wears it with a certain expertise. There's no awkward few seconds as he puts it on. Some guys fumble with it, taking far too long to get the rubber sheath on. He kisses my lips and nipples as he rolls the condom on and in no time at all he's inside me. It's a decent sized cock. Good girth and average length. And it looks handsome. It's a well sculptured cock. No droopy foreskin to contend with. Not my thing. An average head but increasing in girth towards the base. I enjoy it. I enjoy it very much. More than I thought I would. If my butt hole was an ear canal, his penis was the perfect cap to a bic crystal pen. I'm conscious though that I'm closing my eyes a lot. I'm aware I don't want to open my eyes. I do however open them eventually, to acknowledge him. I feel it's only courteous as he's inside me. Once I feel he's reassured, I close them again and let myself go. I'm not sure I thought about it before, but sex is certainly the one activity when I can lose myself entirely.

The sex lasts a considerable amount of time. He fucks me hard, making me jolt each time he thrusts. I am beside myself with pleasure. I wonder if people in loving relationships fuck hard? Do men want to fuck slowly and more tenderly when in love? Is this perhaps one of the reasons sexual chemistry goes when in a relationship? The wildness in sex is omitted out of some kind of ill-placed respect for your partner? I should say — I didn't have this going through my mind as I was being pounded. I thought of it afterwards.

Eventually we collapse, catching our breath. Him more than me, he was doing most of the work. My legs ache from the position they've been in for the length of time. I'm not a spring chicken anymore, certainly not as bendy. We lie down panting, and I'm aware there's hardly any awkwardness. I often want casual hookups out as soon as possible. But we lie there and I feel relaxed and comfortable. *Could he be the one*? I think to myself. I always think this when the sex is hot. That is one thing ticked. *Will we get on*? *Will he listen to me, truly listen when I'm talking*? *Will he have depth to him*? *Will he have passion*? *Will he have a mature head*? *Will he be solvent and manage money well*? *Will he know DIY*? *Will it work*? I ask all these questions anytime there's a moment like this. It feels like I've known him for a long while. A lot longer than just a couple of hours. We talk...it's small talk, which I struggle with normally, but somehow it feels okay with him. I feel him get hard again and we have another hot session. It's even more passionate than the first time. He takes charge. He pays attention to my nipples without me having to telepathically place his hands in my chest area. This is good, this is very good. The tick in this area is big and bold. I smile inside my head. I let myself go again. I come and he doesn't this time. He wants to continue but I don't. I'm all sensitive down there now. The fact that we don't come together has probably taken the boldness off the tick. *If I really, really like the guy, do I try to continue so that he ejaculates too? Do I ensure somehow that we come together?* I think I do, something to think about. My brain will like that.

I think I hear snoring, but I'm not sure. I observe the guy who has just fucked me twice and it doesn't look like he noticed. Perhaps he's partially deaf. He stares at me. There's a glint in his eye. It's clear that he likes me. It's possible he'll want to see me again and I'm okay with that. My neurone network has only just transported this message and he asks if he can come back later. I say sure, thinking to myself that the other guy in my bedroom would have woken up and gone by then.

We eventually dress and go down the stairs. I ask if he would like a drink and he asks for water again. He kisses me and it's okay, still no awkwardness. There's still the feeling of having known him for a long time. This is good, I tell myself. Possibly worth taking the risk of having someone in the next room. I ask his name and he confirms it's the name he has on his Grindr profile, as do I. He says he'll look forward to seeing me again later that evening, and I say that to him too. He leaves. I go back up to my room and open the door quietly. The other guy is still sound asleep. He has moved under the covers now, and is in a foetal position. It kind of pleases me that he trusts me so much to fall asleep in my bed. A total stranger's house. There is no worry on his face, just calmness, and I notice contentment. In slumber it doesn't matter what you may have been up to — Drugs and sex with a stranger — In your sleep you still look peaceful and innocent. Like a baby. It calms me, watching him sleep. I stand there and smile. I don't feel any guilt from having had someone else to have sex with. This guy who snores quietly in my bed most likely just needed somewhere to crash, having partied all night. In some way, I was pleased he chose and trusted me to do that. No qualms, I had had sex with someone else. All is good in the hood. I shut the door behind me and go to get on with some chores around the house.

After a few hours the guy comes down the stairs. He apologises for falling asleep and I tell him there's nothing to apologise for. *I had sex*, I think to myself. *It doesn't matter.* I ask if he wants a drink and offer him some juice on his request. He seems really nice. We talk openly. We discuss politics. Extremely crazy time in politics. Trump and Brexit. He listens attentively to me. I like this, I like this very much. Someone paying attention to me is often very good. A chance of "falling in love with" good. But let's face it, not going to happen. This guy is 32 and obviously likes his drugs. I dabbled in the past, so been there and done that. Don't necessarily want to go back to that time. He's also a total bottom with a below average cock.

We talk some more, and again it's really comfortable. Perhaps, I'm just having a period in my life when talking to any stranger feels comfortable. After a couple of minuscule uncomfortable silences, I say I suppose he wants a lift back to his car. He says yes please with a confidence I also like. He seems quite confident for his age. An old soul. I tell him that, and he smiles. I grab my car keys and wonder whether he woke up at any stage to hear me moaning in the other room. I look back at him, inspecting his face. I resign to the fact I may never know. We both walk out the door and I happily drive him back to his car. It's parked in the city centre. We talk some more as I drive and the communication is easy and relaxed. As it often is when there is no expectation or agenda. He thanks me for my kindness and I tell him no problem. In my head I'm thinking please don't worry about it — *I had sex with someone else*. We get to his car and I stop my car for him to get out. He thanks me again and I say no problem and drive off. Pleased with my kindness. Despite anything that happens in my life. I always endeavour to be kind. It's sometimes the one consoling trait I have that reminds me I'm human and gives me a sense of worthiness. My sex life did not accomplish that.

Later in the day, the other guy does return as he said he would and we have sex again and again. Five times to be precise. I remember thinking fondly to myself — *you keep this up and you'll lose weight in no time*. We eventually simmer from the chemistry and sit in the living room to talk. It's easy and comfortable. This is often the case when I'm *not* that into the person. So this leaves some room for concern, but not enough to make me worry. I'm too shagged out and present to be concerned about it, for now at least. If the guy is really fit, I'm often a bit nervous and it becomes a bit more difficult to be present because I'm so smitten. With enough effort and interesting conversation though, I do stop lusting and concentrate on what he's saying, but this is somewhat rare.

He leaves the next morning after another hot session. We both agree that he will come again the following weekend. I giggle to myself with the thought — *Gosh how many times can you come*? Throughout the week we text on What'sApp everyday, he's keen. He has no qualms about this. I like the confidence he portrays. He's very sexual and also has no qualms about that, I also like this attitude. He says he misses being inside me. I'm flattered.

He turns up the following saturday and we have sex four times. In between, we have a nap and have small talk. He says he's amazed how clean I've been consistently. I smile, an 'awareness of my tummy' smile. I notice his eyes, they're quite far apart in his head. Why hadn't I noticed that before? They have an intensity to them. I think they're brown, but I'm more interested in how far apart they are. We later go down the stairs and decide to go for a walk before dinner. On our walk we chat freely and comfortably. On our return, I prepare a mushroom and asparagus risotto. It turns out he loves mushrooms. I'm not entirely sure how authentic that admission is, but I'm pleased anyway. We sit down to eat but not before having some more sex. We select music on YouTube and sit and eat. We get on well, it's easy. I take the mickey out of him and he laughs. I feel able to speak my mind without worry. Also a good sign.

The next day I have plans which I'd already told him about. I planned to meet my friend for lunch and he said he'd go see a friend of his and her two kids. So we both say goodbye and that we'll see each other later in the evening. I have a lovely time with my friends, I always do. I don't think about the guy once, except when I was about to leave, possibly a bad sign. Often I think about the new guy non-stop if I really like them.

I return home and I get a text from him to say he's on his way back. I'm very tired now, all the sex must have worn me out. I try to keep my eyes open as he'll be back in a few minutes. I sit by a window and admire my tropical garden. I watch my newly purchased solar water fountain squirt like mad in the water feature. It's squirting so sporadically, it reminds me of some of the ladies in straight porn. I always found it funny how when preoccupied with sex, I saw sex in everything. Earlier that day, I had noticed how the pistils on my lilies in the kitchen had droplets of sticky substance on their ends. The ends of the pistil are referred to as stigma. I delicately touched one of the stigmas with my finger. The sexually ripened pistils were no different to a sexually ripened cock. The seeping substance at the end was just as gooey, clear and sticky. An aroused precum covered penis. All of nature has its similarities when you look.

I wonder to myself if I was looking forward to seeing the guy again, I wasn't sure. The doorbell chimes. It had to be him. I peel myself off the sofa and traipse across the living room to open the door. It is him. I say hello and return to the sofa where I collapse, muttering how tired I am. I'm conscious I haven't kissed him. I don't have the urge to. I hope he doesn't come over for a kiss, as I'm not in the mood. I'm baffled, I realise I'm not in the mood at all. I did not want sex with him. I wasn't sure if it was just for the time being. I feel something has changed. This has happened before, with someone else. I recognise it. In fact, recently, a lot. Albeit, never to this extreme. I'd already made the decision, it was a no go. But I tell myself to wait. My feelings might change back. Who am I kidding? They never do. I ask if he'd like to watch a film and suggest we watch a comedy.

We both sit down with a cup of tea, which I get up to make. Then we watch Wanda Sykes stand up. It's hilarious and I laugh out loud, tears streaming down my face. He laughs too, but not hysterically like I was doing. He reaches to kiss me and I flinch momentarily. He retreats, rejected and smirks. I feel bad, so I give him a peck. He sits back down and we continue to watch. The comedy finishes and I ask if he'll like to watch something else. I'm now dreading going to bed. The feeling I have hasn't shifted at all. I cannot bare the thought of having sex with him again. How could I have enjoyed it so much before and be put off by it with such finitum in the space of an afternoon? I do wonder whether I'm crazy, which makes me smile inside. I know I'm a little crazy. I had to be, to have survived my childhood with very little hang-ups. The artist Seal got it right when he sang 'We're never gonna survive, unless we get a little crazy.' I console myself with the thought that it's okay to have changed my mind. People fall in and out of love all the time. People divorce all the time. Perhaps not in such a short space of time, but feelings do change. They aren't consistent, I'd made peace with this fact years ago.

He agrees to watch another film. We decided to finish the one we started to watch the night before but had interrupted because we were so horny for each other. *What the hell happened in such a short space of time*? I continue to ponder this thought. I'm pleased that we at least watch another film before I have to face going to bed with him. The plan was that he stayed another day and left the following morning. *How was I going to cope for a whole day with this new feeling of indifference*? I decide not to think about it and settle into the film we were watching. The film ends in over an hour and he says he's going to bed. I had admired this ability of his to feel so comfortable and at home in my house. But alas, this trait had no endearing quality anymore. I say okay and get up to switch off and lock up. Normal evening routine before bed, I'd imagine for most.

I climb up the stairs, dreading having to face him with my new feelings of nonchalance. *Could I pretend for a whole night and day and then send him a text when he's gone? Enlightening him to the fact that I didn't fancy him anymore in a Whatsapp message?*

I walk into the room, feeling an awkwardness in each step. He's under the duvet on the side of the bed he'd claimed since staying over. I get into bed, purposely leaving my pyjamas on. I lie there in awkward silence. I try to make light conversation and jest, to no avail. My newly found feeling of disinterest stays put in my gut. I finally decide to tell him. I've always prided myself on openness and integrity, despite how awkward, this should be no exception.

'I feel disconnected.' I say, certain now that I'm completely detached from whatever we had going for us in the short time. 'Oh, do you?' Is his reply. I confirm that I do and I've no idea why. He says he was conscious that it may have come across he was all about the sex. I tell him it has nothing to do with him, and that he hasn't done anything wrong. It's all me, I tell him. He looks dejected now. I feel bad. He asks for a cuddle. I decline. I try to explain further. I tell him that before meeting him, I had had a string of people I'd been chatting with on various apps, including Words with Friends. All leading to nowhere. I'd met with a few and nothing happened. People didn't often show they were keen. He on the other hand had been totally the opposite, and that was refreshing. It was nice that he acted on what he felt and it was nice to be wanted. I think it blew me away, I tell him. He tells me he's aware that he's shown no depth so far, whilst he's been with me. It has mostly revolved around sex. I tell him it takes two to tango. He asks if there is anything he can do. I tell him it's nice to be able to talk about it, and if he doesn't mind I'd like to continue discussing. I ask if he has ever felt something for someone and in a flash felt nothing. He says he hasn't. I ask if there's a pattern at all that he can identify. I say I'm trying to make some meaning from the experience. He says he'll go home. I say no and that I feel terrible. It's past midnight. It's far two late to embark on a three hour drive. He says he feels he should go. It doesn't feel right to stay, he says.

Before this, he'd said he would sleep in the spare room to which I'd also declined. Convincing him, and me, that I was happy for him to stay with me in my room. I was at least proud we were exploring this situation in conversation. Of course, it was easy for me to chat. I wasn't the one being rejected. Not such a great environment for deep philosophical conversation when you're being rejected. I should know. I had to make peace with an abandonment issue borne from my childhood. I'd only recently realised I'd finally made peace with it. 49 years later.

I say to him that maybe I'm just too broken to be in a relationship and that it's probably best not to bother anymore, as I found the whole thing excruciating. I'm aware now that I'm in victim mode. It doesn't feel authentic. I'm only saying it to somehow make him feel better. He says not to speak like that and I tell him it's the truth. Another lie. I was trying too hard and I needed to just chill about the whole thing and accept possible loneliness. How many people stay in abusive relationships or relationships where they hate their spouse, just so they did not deal with loneliness? A plenty — I'm quite convinced. So 'chillax'. I tell myself. I've always found a way to look at things positively, despite what I might be going through. Thank god for this grace really. I'm certain I would not have been able to cope with life were it not for this characteristic of mine, that and my little craziness.

My once-again failed encounter gets up to get dressed. I sit up in bed feeling bad, but I'm also looking forward to him leaving. Ambivalence has always been a friend.

"*The one doing the dumping has the issues.*" I remember these words from a book I'd read. I would say it was 50:50 for me in the dumping and being dumped. This consoles me a little. I say to him again that he doesn't have to go and that I was worried about him driving at such a late hour. He says that it's okay and he'll definitely go. I'm torn between my feeling bad, having him leave at midnight, and my feeling bad with him staying. He seems to be very swift in packing. It seems he can't wait to leave either. This consoles me a little. Before long, I get up and go down the stairs. I ask if he's got everything. He says he thinks he has. I give him a hug and he holds me for a while. This is okay. I do sincerely feel sorry about the situation. He says I'm a nice guy and he respects my feelings, and he walks out the door. I ask him to text me when he gets back so I know he got back okay and he says he will.

I close the door — again quietly, I've mastered this door closing business. Part of me wants to slam the door shut, just so the habit is smashed. He would hear it though and wrongly interpret the action. He deserves better than that. I know that'll be the last I see him. I'm determined not to go through this again. No more hookups for a while, I tell myself. Porn will have to suffice. The lesser of two evils. Whatever.

I think we all must accept that 'eating gremlin' inside of us all, called 'loneliness.' We must do away with societal pressure to be in a relationship. Why? Because people are more likely to end up with the wrong person. Couples need to stop taking pity on people that are single. It's all about the connection. By being in relationships it fulfils that need in us all to connect. That connection reduces the appetite of our gremlin. But here's the thing. Perhaps those that have lived single for a long time, have figured out a way to make peace with their loneliness. Acknowledging that at the end of the day, we're all alone, whether you're in a relationship or not.

I would argue that the mastering of this in our mind is much better over all. That way if ever left single again, it shouldn't matter as much. Let's face it, divorce rates are still high, if not increased. If we have friends or family or both, and can connect authentically with loved ones in our life. Then this is something to be grateful for. Even better, if we have mastered our own minds to the point where we can sit our gremlin down, and have an honest open loving chat  with it. Something more likely to achieve when single, then we would have risen above loneliness. So those of you in relationships, think about that before you go pitying people that are single. And help stop us getting into crazy situations like the one I just told you about.

## POOL INFLATABLES

Hi, I'm Ashley. I'm a pretty standard dude...Look at me sounding American. I'm a standard lad. 6ft tall. Dark hair and somewhat bushy eyebrows. I have dark brown eyes. Dark enough to be mysterious. A good thing really as I believe I'm mostly an open book. I have permanently tanned skin. Mixed race you see. Mexican and British. I have a job I'm passionate about. I work in recruitment. I like partying, although I don't go out a lot these days. I mostly work — I guess I'm a workaholic. In my free time I love the gym. I like to keep fit. I probably watch too much television. I know for sure I'm always doing something with my phone, ain't we all?

I'm quite a normal guy, I'd say. It's just that I have what some would say is a weird fetish. I don't personally find it weird — No different to playing with sex toys. I mean, there is no line drawn to what can be a toy for sex is there? I'll just spit it out. I feel nervous now. Okay... I like to wank, fuck and piss on pool inflatables. There — I said it. I like the feel of the plastic. I love the smell of piss. Sometimes the inflatables burst and then I can wank off with the deflated plastic. It's such a lovely feeling, it properly turns me on. I wish others could see it. I can come again and again. The feeling of the plastic on your dick is amazing.

They don't have to be any particular colour. The inflatables I mean — In case you're wondering. Although I suspect you're not wondering about the colour at all. I suspect you're probably dumbfounded. That tends to be the normal reaction I get. No one ever wants to hook up with me. I don't know what the problem is. It's not like I'm hurting anyone. A unicorn may burst now and again, but they don't care. They're plastic!...Well, PVC to be precise. Anyway, before you judge me, let me tell you a story. It might make you understand.

Twenty years ago, I had just moved into a new house in a trendy neighbourhood. I was determined to make an effort and acquaint myself with as many of my neighbours as I could. I didn't want to live somewhere and not know my neighbours. Much better to know people in your neighbourhood so you can ask or borrow something in an emergency. What if I needed some milk in the middle of the night? Or say an egg or paracetamol for an emergency pastry or headache. I will know my neighbours and we will look out for each other. That was my vision and I was going to make it happen. So I invited new neighbours round for dinner, and also took plants and homemade cakes to welcome new homeowners to the area. I'd say at least eighty percent responded positively, reciprocating. I was making my vision a reality.

I first met him when I took some homemade cake to a neighbour who was also an ex work colleague and friend. I live in Buckingham by the way. He had just moved into my friend's house as a lodger. French with long brown wispy hair. Puppy, come-to-bed hazel eyes. A charismatic, alpha male. Drop dead gorgeous and short. I was instantly attracted to him. I made pleasant conversation — I was on a roll. I'd just been round my immediate neighbour's house with some casserole I'd made the day before. I was feeling great from my community service. I introduced myself. He shook my hand and told me he was called Sebastian, ending his vocals with a killer smile.

His smile did something to me. We instantly became friends and he came round the next day for dinner. We spoke openly which is when I told him I was gay. He was straight. He listened so attentively. I had never had that experience from anyone before. It was as if there was no one else in the world but the both of us. He listened, not just with his ears, but with every fibre of his being. I instantly liked him. I think I actually fell in love with him. But I never told him that. I compromised by telling him I fancied him.

He reacted so sweetly. He said okay and asked if that would be a problem with us being friends. I said of course not. I wasn't going to miss out on someone that made me feel I was the only person in the world. 'I can park being attracted to you,' I said. 'I'm older and wiser. Fifteen years older to be precise.' He smiled. His smile mocked me. He might be younger but he was certainly wiser. He didn't say that though. He didn't have to. I did most of the talking and he did the listening. It was obvious who was the wisest. I reconciled to the fact that I would often be abashed at his pauciloquy.

I found out he enjoyed swimming and we were lucky enough to have a decent outdoor pool in our neighbourhood. We started going swimming every week. I hated swimming, but I went so I could spend time with him. I was never predatory though. I did manage to park my lust for him to the side and be a good friend. It was mostly easy. He was so attentive. He was also very affectionate, which sometimes made it difficult. Some evenings he stayed over and we would talk until early hours of the morning. He was such a delight to be around.

He had recently returned from West Africa and he brought back with him a Djembe which is a rope-tuned skin-covered goblet drum. He had the perfect stature for playing this drum. And on a few occasions I would watch in awe as he tapped away with his bare hands. I found out later that the word 'djembe' comes from a saying which translates to "everyone gather together in peace." I smile at the irony of this now.

Over the years he introduced me to a small cosy theatre, golf, running, kite flying, amazing pubs on the canal and of course swimming. I introduced him to exquisite cooking, abstract painting, the dark side of Playstation, philosophical discussions and dress sense. We often played chess and squash together and I found out how competitive he was. He would sulk for a while when beaten. I enjoyed beating him. I guess I was competitive too.

We cherished each other. Often it was okay. The 'me fancying him bit,' I mean. Sometimes when he stayed over, it became a little difficult when we went to bed. He used the spare room. I would lie awake in my room for a while fantasising. He was so fucking gorgeous and he was my friend. He would often kiss my forehead before bed. He was so loving and affectionate. I had never experienced such a thing. So it wasn't long before I started to feel cords pulling on my heart. I consoled myself by playing the mother figure somewhat. Cooking for him and generally looking after him anyway I could. He was always thoughtful. Always wanting to watch what I wanted to watch on telly. He saw the joy it brought me when he knew it was my favourite film.

One of the most memorable days was when we played a duo game on PS4. It was so much fun. Then we went out into a field across the road from the house and flew a kite. There were part gale force winds, so it was a challenge to keep the kite from being ripped up. We laughed so hard that day. In the evening we got a bit tipsy. We cuddled up on the sofa to watch a movie. It was a somewhat drowsy experience. Felt my heart strings tweaking now and again. But I managed to ignore them. He was like a friend, a younger brother, and a lover all rolled into one. Was that even possible. I left the lover part of him outside though, knocking. I refused to let him in.

Every other weekend, we'd both catch the train and he'd take me to the best restaurants in London and it was often a romantic setting. Candle light and live bands. I questioned this now and again. It was a French thing, he would say. He would sometimes feed me from his fork when he wanted me to taste a dish he'd chosen. He did this not only when we were both alone, but in party groups too. He wasn't fazed at all by what people may think. I loved him more for this. He also ate very slowly, always savouring his food. I copied and did the same. We had discussions on all kinds of subjects. He always listened with his whole being. The space he created allowed me to speak with more confidence than I'd ever imagined. I was happy to return the favour and listen to him. We had the most amazing few years.

A few years later, things changed. He had gotten a new job and a girlfriend, and moved to London. Whilst we still stayed in touch, it wasn't as frequent. I was happy for him. I wanted him to be happy. So it was fine. I loved him.

Years went by. We stayed in touch on the phone at least once a fortnight and we met up at least once a month. His girlfriend eventually dumped him. He was visiting me at the time. He had told her he wanted to spend more time with me as he missed me. She hadn't liked that. I tried to console him via texts and phone calls. He stuck his head into his work, possibly like most alpha males would do. He worked in food distribution and supply.

I planned a trip to America for both of us, to cheer him up. We both went and stayed with a friend of mine in San Francisco. I secretly also planned a trip to Vegas from San Francisco for a weekend. He was so surprised when I revealed it to him. We had the best time. On the last night, we got brain fucked on tequila. This was after watching the many hotel attractions on the street for free. They were spectacular, some out of this world. You could tell they were very expensive. Yet every now and again, you'd see a beggar on the street with no footwear and infected feet. Crazy society.

We staggered back to our hotel room, dodging lamp posts on the way. That was the night I sucked his cock for the first time. Cliché I know — Drunken gay and straight guy. He wanted me to, and I very much wanted to. It was not long before he came. In my mouth. I never swallow usually, but this was Sebastian. I had fantasised about this for over 7 years, never believing it would ever happen and being okay with that. I enjoyed his company so much as a friend, it didn't matter. I had dated guys. He'd dated women. But we always made time for each other. One of the reasons I would never have come on to him, despite him being straight, was that I didn't want to ruin possibly the best relationship I'd ever had with another human being.

'Your cum tasted vile.' I say to him, grimacing.

He smiles and hands me a glass of water. Sweet as ever. Not the water. Him. He asks if I'm okay. I say yes. I decide not to tell him I feel a bit subdued. He says he won't necessarily want that to happen again. But he's okay with it, the once. I say okay. He kisses my forehead and we turn over and go to sleep.

The next morning he wakes me up. Cheery as ever. Bike ride, he says. Bike ride, I repeat, my head banging like an orchestra of Djembe drums. This will be so much fun, he says. I feel a bit awkward, but I'm pleased he doesn't seem to be at all. It will be fun, I say, and force a smile. I get up to brush my teeth. Need to get the remnants of tequila and cum out of my mouth. We take no time at all in getting ready. He's straight, probably to be expected. I'm gay, probably not to be expected.

We have a continental breakfast in the restaurant and we converse like nothing awkward happened the night before. We drink a lot of juice. We both have a hangover. Finally we go out to get our hired bikes. Biking is not a common activity in Vegas. When we get outside into the roasting sun we quickly realise why. I'm quite sure the tarmac on the road is melting. I stare at Sebastian with concern. C'mon, he says. I follow reluctantly. Once we start pedalling it's a bit bearable, as there's a light breeze.

After about 40 minutes of biking we pull up at a bar and we get ourselves a drink to hair the dog. We discuss the origin of the phrase — 'Hair of the dog that bit you.' We both agree it's a weird expression, as it relates to the old belief that consuming the hair of a rabid dog that has bitten you, could cure you. It has nothing to do with alcohol.

'Do you want to talk about last night?'

He touches my hand and looks me straight in the eyes and smiles.

'If you want,' I mutter, also with a smile.

He says that it was bound to happen sooner or later. He doesn't regret it happening and it makes him feel closer to me. I smile some more.

'I do not want it to happen again though,' He continues.

'Sure,' I say. 'We were drunk. I never wanted it to happen either. I'm just grateful it doesn't seem to have caused any damage.'

'Not at all,' He says, still touching my hand.

In no time, we lose ourselves in a completely unrelated subject of conversation.

The following day, back at the San Francisco airport, having flown back from Vegas, I'm grouchy. He hands me an energy bar. He always has one in his pocket to give to me when I get hangry. I smile as I take the muesli bar. I quickly unwrap it and take a huge bite.

'Thanks,' I say, oats flying out of my mouth.

'You're welcome,' he smiles.

We were both being extra sensitive and kind. We had had an argument whilst we waited for the plane. Well, not an argument as such. When I lost it and started shouting in anger, he often stopped saying anything and just listened till I'd finished venting. I told you he was the wise one. We only ever had heated discussions three times in the seven years of friendship. Not bad. The argument was over something petty. He was tired and I was hungry and tired.

On the plane, he had looked at me with those puppy eyes and pleaded to me with them. He wanted to lay his head on my shoulder and go to sleep. I said okay. No sooner had he laid his head on my shoulder, I started to get a hard on. I took a deep breath and willed my erection away with a random thought. I adjusted and settled into watching a movie.

He was well rested and less irritable. I was hungry and also still tired. Sebastian knew this when he gave me the energy bar. Like I said, very thoughtful.

In no time at all, my friend arrives to pick us up from the airport in San Francisco. We return to the UK the next day. It was one of the best holidays I'd been on. We visited the Grand Canyon too, when we were in Vegas. It was a long drive, but worth it. We had both sat on the edge of one of the cliffs, dangling our feet. We had watched the sunset. Cliché I know, but it was fucking spectacular. Also free, like the hotel attractions. This time though, no beggars around to taint the experience.

When back home, we're distracted by work and other stuff and we don't see each other for a while. Eventually, though, he texts me asking to meet. He drives up from London. He suggests we go swimming in the community pool and then go for something to eat. I agree. On a Wednesday the pool is open till late. 10pm to be precise. It's also normally quiet.

He suggests we get high on cannabis, which we smoke in a secluded part of the pool. It's a small room where they keep all the inflatables. There are blown up unicorns and flamingos and basic swim rings. No one is around. We keep the door open so we can scout, just in case. We chat and laugh. He gets up to go to the pool. I stay put, smoking the joint, watching the shrubs around the pool. There are some amazing coloured flowers on some of them. The pot must be taking effect.

Sebastian power-swims back and forwards in the pool. He gets out after a few minutes. He stands and looks at me. He has the perfect physique, even the water droplets take delight in caressing down his body. He has defined inguinal ligaments. The muscle around the front of the waist that leads to the pubic region. A friend of mine once referred to them as 'cum gutters.'

He walks over to me. My heart races. I'm throbbing hard now. I want it to go down. This is awful. Please go down, I telepathically try to communicate with my penis. He's going to see my erection in my swimwear. I turn around to hide my bulge. He walks in, and throws himself on the bunch of pool toys. One of them bursts.

'Sebastian!' I shout, glad for this incident, as my penis is almost flaccid again. He turns to me.

'Give me that,' he says.

I pass him the joint.

'Don't get ash on the inflatables,' I say rolling my eyes. Playing mother as I often do in these situations, so as to distract myself.

My hard on has subsided completely now. I'm pleased. He shifts himself nearer me so his crotch is almost in my face. I'm certain he doesn't do this deliberately, but still. He lies back and takes another drag of the joint. I see his bulge. It's too much. My heart kick-starts into a race again. I reach for his cock. He immediately flinches.

'What are you doing?'

'This,' I say, and I remove his cock from his swimming trunks.

I don't know where I got the courage. We had never been high together before. We both don't normally smoke marijuana. He looks cross. I put his cock in my mouth. My heart is racing so much, like a high speed train going berserk in my chest. I feel it might explode; my heart that is.

'I don't want this,' he mumbles.

His cock says otherwise. I continue to suck. I've lost all my faculties. I don't care about the repercussions. I'm high and horny and Sebastian is irresistible.

He gets up in annoyance. He turns me around on my front and closes the door to the room we're in. He does it quietly. He takes his swimming trunks off and spits in my bum hole. He then forces his cock into me. He grabs my neck as he fucks me. I'm sure this is verging on rape. But I like it. He pounds me on top of the inflatables. Another one of them bursts. He doesn't last long at all. He comes in me, and when he pulls out, he notices I'm dirty. 'Putain de merde,' He swears in French. French people use this when they're really vexed. I found out afterwards that it meant 'Whore of shit.' An apt expression I guess.

I turn around and start to wank. I'm so turned on. My whole body has been ignited with Sebastian, it seems. The fact that I was dirty doesn't bother me. There's hardly any smell. Perhaps I'm so turned on, my sense of smell has been overridden.

He stands and watches me with what only looks like vehemence. He tries to wipe his soiled cock. I continue to wank, looking at him. He then does something I did not expect. He starts to piss on me. He pisses all over me as I wank off. I shoot my load. I cum so much my balls hurt. I don't believe I've ever come as much. The inflatables are now covered in piss and cum. I lie there exhausted, trying to catch my breath. He turns around, opens the door and leaves. I never hear from him again.

To say I fell into depression would be an understatement. For almost a year, I struggled to sleep and eat. I couldn't even masturbate. It was as if after that unfortunate day in the room by the pool, nothing aroused me. I'd never been turned on so much in my life. Now I had no interest in sex whatsoever. Like a Panda in captivity. It was bizarre.

I heard from someone that also knew Sebastian. Apparently, he'd moved to Australia with a new girlfriend. I would always feel sad losing his friendship. I try not to blame myself too much though. He was the one that got us the cannabis to smoke. I blamed it all on that. There's no way I'd have done what I did if I was sober. I knew that like I know the veins on my cock. He had been very clear, he didn't want it again and I'd broken that trust.

I buried my head in work. I couldn't play with my Playstation or indeed fly my kite. It was just too sad. I would find prose that I'd written about him. About how much I treasured his friendship. How he was like a mirror enabling me to always be a better version of myself. He'd called me his soulmate several times. He'd always been supportive of me. Helping me to purchase my first piano. I still played that. Thinking about him still brings tears to my eyes now. I stayed in the area I lived in as I'd only just bought my house. Otherwise, I might have buggered off to India or something. I think that's what people do when they're heartbroken.

One day, perhaps about 14 months since I last saw Sebastian, I decided to go swimming for the first time since the event. I did back strokes. The one style I prefer, as it's not necessary to put my head under water. I hate that so much. As I swam, I looked towards the room where it all happened. The evening when Sebastian walked out on me, leaving me drenched in sperm and urine. I had taken all the toys out of the room and hosed them down. Then I'd carefully put them back in, arranging them the best I could. I had discarded the two burst ones. I remember liking the feel of the plastic.

I got out of the swimming pool and walked towards the room. My heart raced. I felt my cock swell in my pants. I felt excited. Not been aroused for over a year. The closer I got to the room, the faster my heart raced and the harder my cock became. I walked into the room and closed the door behind me. Pleased it was a Wednesday evening.

So now you know. Maybe you still judge me. Maybe you don't. Honestly…I don't really care. I get aroused by pool inflatables. So fucking what?

## A CUP FULL OF…

Hi…I'm an escort. I'm afraid I can't tell you my real name. Professional habit. You can call me AJ. I'm a Gemini and I think my Chinese horoscope is a rat. I'm not going to describe myself, just in case. I'd say I'm easy on the eye, and leave it there. I offer services to other gay men. Well…I should say men and leave it at that. I fulfil their fantasies and fetishes. Pretty much anything they need really. Lots of weird shit you wouldn't believe. Everything has a price. Most of my customers don't want vanilla sex. If they wanted that, they'd do it with their partners. Makes sense really, when you think about it. Not that my customers all have partners but I'd say about 50% do. And in that 50% I'd say 25% of those were married men. To women. Yes that's right. Supposedly straight men come to me for sexual pleasure too.

I don't always have to offer sexual pleasure. As in…I don't have to suck cock, fuck or get fucked or wank them off or let them suck or wank me off. At times, I've done the most bizzare things to turn my customers on. I prefer that, it means I don't have to switch off my brain during sex. I learnt to do this you see. Perhaps having bipolar helped, not sure. I was diagnosed with that at an early age.

I had to switch off because some of the men that came to me were so gross — Fat and ugly. Their sweat dripping on you as they thrusted. Only some of the guys though. Some have been really fit. Surprising huh? I would say 50:50. Sometimes the men that come to me just want me to whip them. They sometimes bring their own whip. I would tie them up on the bed and flog the hell out of them, till their backs were raw. I mean, this did not bother me. Sometimes my arm ached afterwards, but better that than my arse.

These men paid the most. They were often in high-powered jobs. I guess being whipped de-stressed them somehow. I never asked. In fact often, there was no talking. Unless of course dirty talking was the thing that got them off. The customers I've had so far have been so precise with what they want. Very clear. Damn good communicators. Via text, I mean. They would type exactly what they wanted. How they wanted it. The frequency of what they wanted. Intensity. Etcetera. Very clear indeed. If only people could be that clear with what they wanted from a relationship!

Recently, a guy paid me £50 to kick him in the balls. I had asked how hard, in a text. He had replied — no limits. When he arrived at my hotel room, I was shocked to see how arrestingly handsome and young he was. He had sent me a picture, but you can never tell from pictures. Or at least I can't. I always requested a picture. Some would send pictures of themselves like 10 years ago. Silly really — What's the point? Taking the risk of me hiking the price when they get to me. Or indeed sending them away.

I knew immediately it was going to be difficult to kick this guy in the balls. It would have been easier if he was an ugly fat bastard. I'd have kicked with all my might then. Pay back for all the obese horrible men that had dripped sweat on me during sex.

I took my leg back all the way and kicked him hard. I'm quite certain I still held back a bit though. He instantly dropped to the floor and went into a foetal position. Holding his balls, he ejaculated in his pants. I guess I kicked him perfectly. I stood and watched him orgasm on my hotel room floor. Oh yea...I didn't tell you. I would pay for a travel lodge for the weekend. That way customers did not come to my home. Less risky that way. Although, I felt confident I could look after myself if someone wanted to try something. I'm quite street wise you see. I had to be. You can't learn that at school. I will come back to that later. Let's go back to the guy rolling around on my hotel room floor. Holding his balls.

I wanted to ask him where it all started. I was dying to ask him where it all started. But I guessed he would have asked for his money back. If he wanted to put himself in a position where he might be judged. Then he might as well have got a mate of his to kick him in the balls. He paid me for the privacy. No questions asked. No judgement. Again, makes sense when you think about it. I wondered how much he would charge to reveal the 'whys' though.

The guy eventually got up off the floor. Took out the payment in notes and left it on the side table. He didn't look at me. He opened the door and ventured out into the hallway. Another satisfied customer.

I guess you're dying to know how I got into this line of work. Well…grab yourself a cuppa and I'll tell you.

I was one of two siblings. My sister was older by 5 years. My dad left when I was very young. My mum was an alcoholic. She beat me...A lot. I think I reminded her of my dad and she hated him...A lot. My sister tried to stop her but our mum was fucking strong when she was pissed on vodka. It was like vodka gave her super powers. Some days I would go without food, just so I kept out of the way. Better to go hungry than be beaten. I would hide away in different rooms. Ones furthest away from my mum. When she went out at night was the worst. She would come in tutting and swearing. Just the sound of the door slam behind her as she entered the house, made me taste bile in my mouth. I was so frightened of her. Sometimes, rarely, she would try to be a good mother. She would attempt cooking. Mostly oven chips and pie. If you were lucky you got peas with it. No wonder I got fat. She could manage about two days of being nice. But eventually her demons would get the better of her. She would go out to find alcohol and come back plastered. Funny, how many words there are for getting drunk. Smashed, Blottoed and Plastered are my favourite. Perhaps sloshed — at a push. But bibulous and maudlin. Who came up with those? Shakespeare probably.

Anyway, I digress. Back to my mum. Bless her. She was a fucking mess! Should never have had kids. She quite literally did not know what to do with us. My sister and I got taken into foster homes eventually. We were separated. No loss. We didn't really get on. I was 13 years old when I was taken to a foster home with 12 children. It was a large dingy building with an oppressive inside. The staff always seemed miserable. I wondered whether they had once been in a foster home. But then why would they want to return, even though it was to work? Desire to make a difference, I supposed. It would have been heart wrenching to tell them they weren't doing a great job of it.

I tried to settle into the foster home. I became proper fat in the process. Kids bullied me at school as well as at the foster home. I was depressed and ate more. Vicious circle. Sometimes I would get really hyper. Talking like I was high. Restless. Getting myself into trouble. Then a few days later I'd be in a slump. Depressed as hell. It was around this time I was diagnosed with Type 2 Bipolar. The bullying got worse.

I made a decision to do something about it. In my world you had to toughen up. And fast. It's survival of the fittest. If you're going to be like… *Aww mum didn't love me. I'm being bullied. Poor me. Bi Polar. Boohoohoo.* You might as well get in your box and be done with it. Bullies sniff out vulnerable victim vibes, like flies sniff out roadkill.

Primal instincts took over. I figured out a way to help in the kitchen preparing the food. One day the bully was picking on me as he did. I haven't described or named him because I can't remember him. Wiped clean from my memory. Maybe being bipolar helped with that too. If so, good. The bullying normally involved pinching and pushing me around whilst laughing. Calling me fatty. I picked up the courage to push him against a wall, using my fat to keep him in place. I spoke firmly but calmly down his ear hole, telling him if he didn't stop, I was going to put shit in his food. He knew I worked in the kitchen. He looked into my eyes — He knew I meant it. He left me well alone after that. That's one thing I noticed. It seemed all of us in the foster home had an understanding. Our instincts seemed sharper. A hard, tough life did this to you I reckon. All of us knew deep down we were capable of anything to survive. We had nothing to lose. This is where I honed being streetwise.

Despite being able to stick up for myself, I started self-harming. When I had my lows they were pretty bad. I would find a sharp object and cut the side of my waist several times. It gave me a sense of release. Made me feel something. I had had to switch off to be able to cope with my situation you see. But now and again I needed to feel something. Can't cheat nature I suppose, we are feeling creatures of habit. Physical pain was as good a feeling as any. In the kitchen there was always some broken crockery. I would offer to clear up and keep a nice sharp piece for myself. I'd often sit in a toilet cubicle and cut myself slowly, savouring the sharp sweet pain. I would watch the blood seep out. A glorious rich, bright red. I would dab the cut with toilet paper when the drip was just about to touch my shorts or trousers. Then I would watch again as the blood seeped, partly hypnotised. Looking back now it was the best meditation. I was always present. After a few minutes I would disembark from the cubicle. Feeling rather chilled, albeit with a dull nagging pain in my side.

One day, my sister got in touch. Even though we were like chalk and cheese, it was really good to hear from her. Not so good to hear what she was telling me. She reported that she had left school. She hated the shoes she had been given by social services. Apparently they were hideous and all the other teens laughed at her. She had just turned 17 and she could do what she wanted. I thought she was stupid to leave school just because she didn't like a pair of shoes. But I didn't tell her that. She told me in a roundabout way that she had become a sex worker. I had to play detective to figure that out though. I listened in part shock and awe. It seemed like she knew what she was doing. So I wished her well. Sex worker — A politically correct name for a prostitute. Her disclosure stayed in my head for a while.

I soon turned 17 and I too could choose to do what I wanted. Whilst at the foster home, a couple of dodgy men had approached me in the compound. They asked if I would like to make some money. I always ignored them, never enquiring further. I had started to lose the weight then. Puberty seemed to be doing well with my metabolism. I wasn't that into food any more. I started to burn the fat. I began to notice my body. I definitely noticed my weiner. It had grown considerably. At first I thought it was normal. But when showering with the other lads I soon realised mine was not normal at all. It was longer and thicker. It made me a bit self conscious, but I soon accepted it. I looked up rude names to call it. Yoghurt slinger was my favourite at the time, although mine fitted best with King Dong.

I knew very early on that I didn't fancy girls. I used to get hard in the communal shower with the other boys, you see. I knew what that meant. My dick would never be referred to as a Vagina miner. I also noticed that when I masturbated, I came loads. Again, I thought this was normal until I watched porn. I soon realised my quantity was not normal at all. There was always a lot of it. I mean a hell of a lot.

A week before leaving the foster home, social services had found me a self-contained flat. It was arranged that someone would check in on me twice a day, offering support. A mentor was also allocated to help me with day to day living. It was crazy how much stuff you had to know, moving into your own place. Your utilities and how to pay them. Benefits. House chores. Bin days. Cooking. Laundry. Managing your money. Managing the food in your fridge. Turning things off when finished. Why didn't they teach all that at school instead of quadratic equations? I was keen on cooking proper meals. No more frozen food. My mum's cooking had put me off. I was determined to sort myself out.

One of those dodgy guys approached me again. He looked like a porn star from a 70's porn. He asked if I'd like to make some easy money. The word 'easy' got my attention. I decided not to dismiss him this time. I asked what he meant and he told me. I asked him again because I could not believe what I was hearing. He repeated himself. He had definitely told me what I heard. I got excited. It *was* going to be easy money. Very easy money indeed. I just needed to get myself a fridge freezer and a microwave. He pulled out a handful of scraps of paper from his trousers pocket and gave me one of them. It had a telephone number on it.

The next day was moving day. The social worker and mentor were helping me get bits of furniture. I stressed that, more than anything I needed a fridge freezer and a microwave. They promised they would sort me out with a bed, fridge freezer and a microwave. They asked why I had asked for a microwave and not a cooker. They reminded me that I'd always said I wanted to cook meals from scratch. I said I would like a cooker too. I wanted both. They both said fair enough. I was ecstatic about moving into my own place. I was even more excited about starting to make easy money. I couldn't believe my luck. I guess God finally took pity on me.

Moving in was a bit of a pain, but excitement over my new lucrative business venture made it bearable. My social worker and mentor were a great help. My bedroom looked a decent size. The few clothes I had were on the floor for now. My mentor was looking to get me a wardrobe from 'freecycle'. (a website where people offered stuff they didn't want any more for free). My bed was a double bed which I was grateful for. When my fridge freezer and microwave arrived, I actually got a stiffy. I had to leave the kitchen to conceal it somehow. The social worker asked if I was okay. I replied, was more than okay and thanked him again. I said this while tapping the tip of my willy so it went down.

My social worker was a good man. Short hair. Clean shaven. Quite thin. Bony face. Big hands, like flippers. Kind, gentle light brown eyes. He had helped me so much. My mentor seemed okay too. He had a bit more weight on him. Bald head. Stubble. Fat face. Deep set dark brown mysterious eyes. He reminded me of one of my teachers.

In the evening, after all the sorting and unpacking, they ordered a take away. I stuffed the noodles into me as I had plans. They asked me to slow down. I said I wanted to go to bed early as I was knackered. A lie. They put telephone numbers on the new mobile phone they had bought me and said they would see me the next day, in the afternoon. I said okay and they left.

I frantically fished for the scrap of paper from the dodgy guy. I called the number and spoke to the man who had visited me when at the foster home. My heart racing, I asked for more info. He told me. I said I could deliver a lot sooner. There was a pause. He asked if I was sure. I said yes. He said okay, three days. I said cool. I confirmed the price. He verified it would be £60. I said cool again and gave him my address. I was a bit nervous doing this. I had just got my new place. Better not fuck it up.

I went straight into the kitchen to find a cup. I got one of two that appeared the right size. I took my jeans and pants down and started to have a wank. It didn't take me long before I shot my load. The word "load" is used way too loosely I feel. It was more appropriate when I ejaculated. It was three days worth as well. I hadn't had time to play with myself with the move and everything. I struggled to aim it in the cup and some spilt. Nonetheless, I almost half filled the cup. Two more goes and it should be full. Might have to call the guy back and rearrange. One day instead of three days. I cleaned the mess I'd made and put the cup of cum in the freezer.

The next morning I woke up early. I'd gone to bed early. Really early for me. I have a raging hard on. Morning glory. I start to have a morning wank in bed. It's always the way, once I remind my cock of the pleasure it can bestow. It only wants more. After a few minutes I'm about to come. Shit. Shit. Shit. I jumped out of bed. Holding the tip of my cock to stop the cum. I staggered into the kitchen and opened the freezer. I grabbed the only thing in it. The cup, almost half filled with semen. I aimed my cock into the cup again. The coldness started to make me lose my hard-on. I searched for my phone. I googled porn. My hard on returned. In no time I started to fill the cup again. Just a little bit more and the cup would be full. I had greatly underestimated just how much I ejaculated. It was quite incredible — Circus incredible. Not a family circus obviously. I took the cup back to the kitchen and retreated to my bedroom to have another lie down. I had a lot to do, but needed some more sleep.

Two days passed by. It had taken me a while to settle into my new flat, but I was getting there. My cup is now full. The guy paying me for it was supposed to come yesterday but didn't turn up. Said he had the flu. I found out what he was going to do with the cum. It made me gag thinking about it. I drank a lot of pineapple juice for the other ejaculations. Someone told me it made your cum taste nicer. He wanted me to first defrost it in the microwave. Then he was going to drink it in front of me. It wasn't enough that he just took the cup and had a sip at his leisure. No... I had to be there and watch. We would make the exchange. Cup full of cum, and I watch him drink it for £60. That was the deal.

A few days later the guy did turn up. He seemed like any normal guy. You would never think that he got off by drinking young lads cum. Perhaps he knew something that others didn't. Maybe it was some kind of Elixir — prolonging life.  It was important that I watched him as he drank it.

When it was microwaved, the smell was vile. I can't describe it. I had to open all the windows in the flat. The guy was impressed when I said that I had his cup ready in just two days. Normally he had to wait at least a week, sometimes two weeks for the cup to be filled. Also, I think he really liked the taste as he offered to pay for more as soon as he'd finished sucking on the cup. I guess the pineapple juice worked.

So now you know how I got into this line of work. I had planned to just stick to filling a cup with cum. It was really easy for me due to the quantity of my semen. But I just couldn't stand the smell when it was microwaved. So I decided to try other things. I was surprised how much people would pay for certain things. Some guys just wanted me to wear my underpants for like a week and then send them in the post. The Japanese refer to this as Burusera. Sexual gratification received from sniffing high school girl knickers. The exception of course is that I'm no high school girl. When I sent mine it was sometimes with a bit of brown or white or both. I was certain it was always with a few droplets of yellow. £60 for sending off my often soiled pants, not including the cost of post and packaging. Again, very easy money.

I did get a job providing care and support for people with learning disabilities. I didn't stay long though. The pay was abysmal. I wondered why the care industry got paid peanuts for doing such a needed job in society. I just didn't get it. I was used to earning a lot more, so I went back to my sex working profession. Eventually, I started exploring other avenues. You could say I kind of got addicted. I started fucking and getting fucked sometimes. Most people — men and women, wanted to try to take my cock due to its size. I charged £100 for an hour. On a weekend I could make £600 to £800, and that was after subtracting the payment for the hotel room. I'd be shattered afterwards though, requiring two days of sleep and rest. But I thought it was so worth it. I'd often do two weekends back-to-back and then have a weekend off.

The worst offer I've had is one guy wanting me to poop in his mouth. I texted to inform him that that would be £400. He declined saying that the going rate was £80 to £120. The 'going rate!' I had to laugh out loud. Thankfully we were texting. I'd say it was important that you didn't judge in this profession. I thanked him and said no thanks. I just couldn't bring myself to squat over someone's open mouth and have a dump.

The best offer I've ever had, which happened a couple of times, was an older gentleman who just wanted me to hang out with him in a restaurant and have dinner. All he wanted was to talk and have someone with him. I felt really sad for him. Paying, just for company. When I got back home, I cried. It was heart wrenching. I had gone over time with him and didn't care. Normally I'm strict with time. After crying I felt at ease with myself. Both for crying and for being company to a really lonely person. I promised to always give my time to customers that wanted this. It was actually nice to talk too.

Having someone actually listen to me. And I got paid. It was a no brainer.

My sister called again. We chatted, but I didn't tell her what I was up to. I'm not too sure why I didn't tell her. Perhaps I thought it was okay with one sibling doing it. Perhaps she had some sense of normality phoning me and talking to me about ordinary day to day stuff. Telling her I was also a sex worker would have ruined her illusion. I decided not to tell her and leave her believing I was working for a mobile phone company. She had so much pride in her voice when I first told her that. I had never heard that in someone's voice before. I wanted to continue hearing that. And I'm sure she wanted to continue believing the lie I told her. It was my gift to her. Well, I suppose my gift to both of us. For a few minutes we could pretend some normality.

It's not all bad. The profession I mean. I learnt to switch off, like I said earlier. And most of the time I just sent underwear in the post or came in a cup. A couple of times some guys wanted me to send them a used condom. As in one I had come in. All I had to do was ejaculate into a condom, take it off, tie it at the end and send it off in a padded envelope to the address stated in text. Easy — Except taking the condom off without it spilling of course.

I didn't mind being sucked off either. Most of my clients wanted to worship my cock. Which guy wouldn't want their cock worshipped? — And get paid for the convenience. No brainer!

The one thing I didn't do was kiss. I felt that was sacred. I felt I should save that for someone special. I wasn't all that fond of fucking or being fucked either. I do this only when I need a lot of money and fast. You know, like to buy something pricey or go on a holiday. I charged £100. Sometimes £200 if the guy was a real minger. Whether performing as a top or bottom I would always stay on top just in case. I didn't feel too vulnerable then you see. Also if the person sweated a lot, they didn't have to drip all over me.

There was one guy that was insistent he wanted to be on top whilst he fucked me. I tried everything to decline, saying I only ever rode or mounted. He just kept raising the price until I finally gave in. In the end he offered £500 for a 30 minute session. He was good-looking too. Quite soft features to his somewhat rounded face. He just wanted me to lie on my back and he wanted to fuck me. I distinctly remember him being quite nervous. I thought this was a little strange, especially as he had come in with a stiffy in his trousers. Nervousness and hard-ons don't usually go together. Nonetheless, I thought his anxiety was endearing. It made me relax about being on my back. I remember his cock being quite thick. Not rock hard though. Hard enough to penetrate I suppose. His balls were quite small too. There was something rather strange about him — and his cock. I couldn't quite put a finger on it. He seemed quite pleased with himself afterwards. He asked if he could quickly use the bathroom, which he did and then left, thanking me again as he strolled out the door.

I never had anyone stay overnight. And, like I mentioned before, I can look after myself if I need to; apart from my experience in the foster home. Being a doorman for about a year, off and on, gave me a few tips on how to deal with unruly people. To keep tabs on my sexual health I attended the health clinic after every five clients. This ensured I didn't contract any STD's and if I did, it was treated straight away.

I smoke weed sometimes. Helps me escape my reality. Probably not a great idea due to my having bipolar and all, but what the heck. It helps temper the hypomania. I never drank alcohol. My mother put me off that pastime for good. Besides, I didn't want anything making me feel edgy. Get anxious enough as it is.

I get to meet a lot of 'interesting' characters. Don't want to say weird, that will be judging. Learnt not to do that. Although it's very hard not to judge, when someone asks you to fuck a chicken for money. My fingers were stupefied. I had no idea what to text back in response to that one. Didn't even bother asking if the chicken will be alive, dead or straight from Tesco, ready for roasting. Thank god for the block function.

One guy that came to me for sex had down's syndrome. I felt really sorry for him. Where do people with learning disabilities get their sexual needs met? I decided to fuck him at a reduced rate. I also informed him it will be a one off. He agreed and was happy with that. I think he was the one guy that smiled the most after the session.

Another guy that I met with just wanted to suck on my toes. He was into feet in a big way. In preparation I decided to pamper my feet. I never really paid any attention to my feet. And, let's face it, they hold us up. We couldn't get anywhere without them. I bought some scrub and cream just for feet. Cut my toenails. Used the scrub and cream and I doubt my feet had ever looked so good. I have to say when the guy worshipped my feet, it was quite a turn on actually. He massaged and sucked all my toes and then wanked himself off using my feet. Then he sucked me off. I'm indebted to that guy, cause since then I look after my feet more. My feet now get TLC every other month. He taught me to love my feet. This was certainly a step in the right direction to loving myself. Pun intended.

Looking back now, some of my encounters were just so funny. Hilarious even. I was providing a service. Helping people. Whichever way you look at it, I was providing a service for people. Meeting people's needs. Nothing wrong with that, right?

## NAPPIES

Hi, my name is Conrad. I'm blonde with blue eyes. The kind Hitler was trying to conserve as a perfect race. Except, I don't think I'm perfect at all. I have a really small willy you see. It makes me so anxious. I've made up for this tiny appendage, not by owning a giganormous jeep, but by building my muscles to magnanimous proportions. I visit the gym pretty much every day, except when I'm ill. I tend not to use the communal showers in the gym. Mainly because of embarrassment over my manhood. But also because I don't fancy getting verrucas on my feet. I know you can wear flip-flops, but I don't like wearing them. Precisely, because they flip-flop.

Being conscious over my dick became more embedded in my cerebral cortex after a hook up with a woman. She had blond hair and blue eyes. We met at a bar and we seemed to hit it off straight away. I asked her back to mine. She didn't seem the type to be offended by that, not that I'm calling her a slapper or anything, she was just keen that's all.

When we got back to mine, she immediately went for my belt. Perhaps she was a slapper, but she was fit, so I let her. My anxiety started to get the better of me, but I made it look like I was just really into her. She did stop at one stage, looking at me to try and gauge what was happening. Then we started to kiss and she went for my belt again. Tugging at it. I would have thought, based on her actions so far, that she would have been able to take my belt off with ease. I had a theory that a lady willing to go to bed with you on a first meet, would be able to take a belt off with ease. Similarly a guy should be able to take off a bra strap with ease based on the same reasoning. This woman, however, seemed to be stuck with the belt unfastening. Made me wonder. Maybe she wasn't a slut after all and was just acting out. A dare? High on some kind of drug? Or maybe she refused to be conformed into an expectation of her. Maybe she fancied me and wanted sex with me straight away. This is the 21st century after all.

She gave up tugging after a while. Stopped kissing and looked at me. It was easy to read what she wanted. I grabbed my belt and delicately released the prong. I had tightened the belt a lot more than usual, because I was wearing a silk shirt that easily untucked itself. It had a flat bottom hem so could have been worn untucked. But I had to have my shirts tucked in, whether it was flat hemmed or not. Clothes OCD I suppose. Only shirts with flat bottom hems are meant to be worn untucked. I despise these kinds of silly rules. The 'clothes police' could try arresting me if they dared.

The lady, whose name I've conveniently forgotten, resumed kissing me again. I took a deep breath and pulled my hard dick out of my pants. She felt for it, gently pushing my hand away. She held it and stopped kissing abruptly. She opened her eyes and looked down and to my stark horror she burst out laughing whilst letting go of my dick. Anyone would think she had been holding a floppy rubber chick. She did apologise immediately, having witnessed the shock on my face, but she still continued to laugh. I quickly popped my pathetic phallus away.

The woman could not stop laughing. I was glad I'd forgotten her name. She got up from the edge of the sofa and reached for her coat which she had flung on the back of the sofa. She kept apologising for laughing, and all I wanted to do was punch her in the face. I was glad she was making a swift effort to leave. She finally put her shoes back on and said sorry again. She opened the door and left. I remained seated on the sofa. Dejected did not cut it. I always knew my penis was small, but to have someone burst out laughing at it was not expected. Perhaps it was bound to happen sooner or later. I had to admire the woman's audacity. Considering the fact *she* had the smallest penis really. The clitoris. She found it funny — I guess it was funny. Nature was cruel. Why bestow a small penis on a man?

After that rejection episode, I decided to stick to seeing men. I'm bisexual you see. I could be bottom when having sex with men, and that suited me. To hell with women. Despite having mastered the art of cunnilingus to make up for a small penis, most women could not get past seeing the small willy. So I decided to stick to seeing men. Real tops were not too fussed with small cocks. They were mostly interested in the bum. I was blessed with a bubble butt, so I decided to make the best of my assets.

My other pastimes — I should swiftly mention before you think I'm obsessed with sex include: rock climbing, fishing, music — I particularly enjoy the 80's. I do like movies but not more than music. I enjoy going to concerts when I can, although these days I've not been to one for a while. I seem to be less tolerant of stupid people. Lots of them seem to attend concerts. So now I stick to watching my favourite bands perform in concerts — on YouTube. I've already told you I enjoy the gym.

I work as a financial analyst — a career I kind of fell into, really. I studied geography at university, and never did anything with it. But numbers I found I could work with. I mean they never disagree. If I need to make a six a nine, I just turn it around. It's that simple. I'm not too sure I'd say I love the job but I'm very good at it and it pays very well. So as good a job as any I feel. I do work a lot. I guess some would call me a workaholic. Sometimes my job is quite stressful. Or I should say sometimes I allow myself to get stressed. We all use such disempowering language don't we? Our jobs can only be stressful if we let it, surely. I'm going to endeavour to watch my language as I narrate to you.

A few months back, I was working way too much — escape from some repressed sexual calling perhaps. I do wonder now as I tell you this. Anyway, I had a nervous breakdown. My brain literally shut down and I slumped into a darkened chasm of helplessness. Very dilapidating. Scary. There was nothing I could do about it. I just had to ride it. I was given time off work and was housebound for a while. At times like this you wish you had someone living with you. I had a neighbour that checked in on me now and again. I was grateful for that. I mostly slept. Way too much cortisol (stress hormone), had flooded my nervous system and it needed to be flushed out. Our bodies know what they need a lot of the time. And mine needed rest. Lots of it. I packed my fridge with healthy food options and drank a lot of cranberry juice. Cranberry juice just sounded the most healthy of the juices. I felt it would help dilute the cortisol in my system. I don't have any scientific back-up for that reasoning, it's just what I thought and I went along with it. Sometimes you go with a hunch, there doesn't have to be evidence or even a logical reason. Sometimes you just follow your instincts, and my instincts screamed cranberry juice.

I had about four months off work and when I returned, it was with a different approach. I did have moments when I felt overwhelmed. When those moments came, I got up and went for a walk. Recently, I got into something that even shocks me when I think about it. I never really gave too much thought as to how I got into this fetish of mine. Everything I've told you so far, I can't see having any bearing on it. Perhaps some of it does. Maybe a relief of the stress? The small penis dilemma may have something to do with it? The breakdown? But honestly I'm not too sure. I'll let you figure it out. I can't believe I'm about to tell you this. I've never spoken about it to anyone. There's definitely some shame coming up. But isn't there shame lingering with any kind of sex? Slightly out of the ordinary sex. How many straight couples for instance enjoy anal sex but would never ever admit it to anyone, out of some kind of misplaced shame. Well, my fetish is out of the ordinary, that's for sure. I'll just come out with it. To hell with it. It turns me on so…

My fetish is wearing nappies and pretending to be a baby. I believe it's called AB/DL which stands for Adult Baby/Diaper Lover. It's obviously an American acronym. Does that mean it originated in the States? I doubt it. They're just more open about stuff. The British still see sex as taboo. So there was hardly going to be an acronym around sex derived here.

There! I've said it! I'm not harming anyone. I get off by having a guy or a woman change my nappy and treat me like a baby. Some kind of play with faeces is part of the ritual. I do actually poop in the nappy and the guy changes it for me. I pretend to be a helpless baby. Him doing the changing gets him hard and I'm turned on by the ritual of the nappy change. The guy would wipe me clean. There is often the smell of faeces in the air. All part of the sexual atmosphere. He would clean me and put a new nappy on me. The whole time I lie down being helpless and vulnerable. The dynamic of that and him being in charge is the attraction I guess. I'm indebted to him. You cannot be more vulnerable than lying with poo in a nappy and getting changed. It would sometimes lead to the guy fucking me, but this was very rare. I remember one guy making a hole in the nappy and fucking me with the nappy on. This was particularly pleasurable.

Most men are happy with the role play taking ages. I'm not too bothered either way. If he does decide to penetrate me, at least I don't have to bother with douching. How on earth did all this start? I hear you asking in possible desperation to try and understand. Well, Like I said I'm not too sure, but I'll start from my childhood. Dah Dah! Doesn't it always start from our childhood? I'll do my best to narrate carefully my entire childhood and perhaps you, *and* I for that matter will figure it out. Mostly, I guess, it may just pique your interest in the subject.

I was born in a little village in Europe. I'm not going to be any more specific than that because I don't want you prejudging already. Making assumptions like we all do. It was a little village and we were a little family. My mum and dad worked a lot. And my little sister and I had a nanny look after us a lot when we were little. Hold back from making conjecture...god! We can't help ourselves, can we? Just stop the cogs turning for a few minutes and take in what I tell you without any judgement. At least until the end. I think it will be clearer that way. Okay?

Okay… like I said, small working family, small village, me and sister. So far, so good. I can't remember much of my childhood as it happens. I have glimpses of memories. My mum staring at me whilst in the car on a family trip, with my dad driving. The memory I have is vague. My mum just stares at me, which is very odd. The other memory is me in primary school. I'm in the playground, and I'm alone. I think I feel sad, but I can't be sure. Everyone else is playing in groups, and I'm sitting in a corner on my own. And that's it, I think. Quite odd memories I'd say.

Oh, I do also remember playing pretend house and family. Me pretending to be a baby whilst my sister pretends to be mum. I had a feeding bottle and my sister was checking and fussing over me. That's interesting, I'd forgotten about that. Memory is a funny thing, huh? Anyway, fast forward a bit. We were okay as a family, as far as I remember, even though we had a babysitter and nanny a lot of the time. At the time I never thought this was strange. But you know, as I think about it, I can't remember my mum ever hugging me. I guess I've just forgotten. She must have hugged me. I just can't remember.

Earlier today, before you turned up for the skype interview, I decided to rummage for some old pictures of me as a child. I found a few. Well, three to be precise. I noticed something I hadn't before. I wasn't smiling in any of the pictures. My mum looked like she was happy for someone to take me off her hands. I know what you're probably thinking. Postnatal depression? Honestly...I'm not sure. I never heard anything about that from my dad or sister.

I didn't have sex till I was 25 years old. I think that's quite old. Yes… partly it was to do with the size of my penis. I was embarrassed to have anyone see it. *I* didn't want to see it. So I suppressed my sexual urges for a long time. I read somewhere that doing that can cause sexual deviancy. So there you go, perhaps it was just that. It doesn't pay to suppress or refuse *any* of your human needs. It's just expressed in other more profound ways. Denying your sexual needs has never turned out well throughout history. You just have to look at the Catholics!

I'm really pleased you're interviewing me about this fetish. I'm finding it quite cathartic. Slowly putting together the jigsaw puzzle. But most importantly making peace with any bit of shame I harbour inside —Thank you.

The first time I ever thought I was into nappies? Hmmm — I guess that wasn't too long after my nervous breakdown. Like I mentioned earlier, I did sometimes get very stressed with work. Silly I know. Eventually, your body has to take charge and shuts down just so you see sense. I guess I was lucky I didn't have a heart attack and die.

When I was resting up at home, having been discharged from the hospital, most days I just wanted to stay in bed and not move. Not even to the toilet. On one of those days I decided to wrap myself in a really soft blanket. It was given to me by a dear friend who I unfortunately don't see any more. She was Romanian and got together with a Romanian guy. He turned out to be very possessive and jealous and he didn't want her seeing me as a friend any more. Apparently most Romanian men are like this.

Anyway, I treasure the blanket she gave me, even now. It was a Shilucheng Fleece soft warm fuzzy plush lightweight twin soft blanket. I wrapped it around myself tight, tucking it into my genitals and around my waist, somehow restricting myself. I found it immensely comforting. I fell into the most comforted slumber. I woke up bursting to go for a wee. I was so comforted I didn't want to get up and have to unwrap myself from the fleecy heaven I was in. I decided to pee in the bed. I did — and was present to the radiating warmth I felt as I urinated. The feeling was intense. I don't know if it was the combination of the blanket and the fact I was still sleepy. But the gratification I derived from it — I just can't explain it to you. It was such an amazing feeling. The heat, diffusing around my crotch and lower abdomen. It was possibly the most pleasure I'd ever had in that area. It actually made me hard. That is when it all started for me.

Like I said before, it isn't always sexual. In fact for me it very often isn't. Some men want to fuck, as it turns them on. When with women they often just want to mother me. They don't tend to be interested in sex. I do know people...well men mostly, never known women to be into AB/DL. The men have all sorts of reasons why they become adult babies. Some just want to relinquish all control. These men are often in high-powered jobs. What better way to relinquish control than to put yourself in a nappy and wee and poop yourself? Relying on someone else to change you. For some, me included, it is sheer bliss. Some people are keen to show it in public though, which I'm not. Not a fan of being ridiculed. For some that is the turn on. Being dehumanised, humiliated etc. For me it's just the feeling and the act of playing out being a baby and letting someone care for me. That's what I love. For some autistic fella it's again the sense of comfort and stress relief it provides. Perhaps I'm a bit autistic. We're all on the spectrum after all. There is online shopping now that caters to the needs of adult babies. It's a growing industry, believe it or not. Gives you an idea how many of us there are out there.

Anyhow, over the last couple of years, I've not been stressed out once. I still do the same job and continue to be good at it. Do I owe this to wearing nappies? Well, I didn't embark on some master self development class or read a groundbreaking bestseller on how to eliminate stress. So it's difficult not to give nappies all the credit for the stress free life I now lead. I can't imagine my life without wearing nappies now. I don't have shame. I find it strange that you can feel shame in something that makes you feel pleasure. I can't honestly understand that mentality, and to deny yourself pleasure is just plain stupid in my opinion. Hopefully, paedophiles won't agree with that sentiment!

I did have a steady woman that I cohabited with for a while, which was nice. I wasn't really into the sex thing with men if I was honest. I got my pleasure purely from the role play. Didn't need penetrative sex of any description to satisfy me. Was this some kind of subconscious rebellion against the use of my penis? Who knows. I just know I'm content. Isn't that all we want at the end of the day? To be content? We all do what we have to do to navigate this life. So long as we're not harming anyone, then I really don't see that there's an issue. Do you?

# ADDICTION

Hi there, I'm Hamish Smithereen. I'm 5ft 8ins with a lift to my ankles when I walk. I guess subconsciously I'm trying to make myself taller. It could be that it's just the way I walk, but you make of it what you want. I have green eyes, not quite like emeralds, but perhaps like the colour of the beaches around Crete. I pride myself in the knowledge that they are the most uncommon eye colour in the world. 2% to be precise. I have a defined jawline, which I think makes me desirable to anyone that takes a fancy to me. My shoulders aren't broad as such, but I make up for this with a hairy chest. I used to be outgoing, gregarious and a kind of party animal. Enjoying socialising and hosting dinner parties for friends. I enjoyed it very much, until something happened that evaporated that life for me. You see, I presently have agoraphobia. I never in a million years would have thought I'd be trapped in my internal fears. I never was one to play the victim card. Not any more than the average person anyway; where having a self-pity party and inviting all your demons to tea was okay now and again — Having it last an evening at a stretch.

I've had agoraphobia for almost a year now. It's dreadful. I've squeezed every bit of reason and positivity out of it though. Writing music and poems and novellas. Also painting with acrylic on canvas. I've made the best of it, though it still doesn't take away the fact that I'm trapped and unable to go outside. I know it's pathetic, but there you are. Grab yourself a hot or cold drink, then sit back and let me tell you what happened. It will be cathartic for me to share with a complete stranger, and you will hopefully be surprised and enlightened by a good story.

I guess I should go back to when I was young. Very young. I have two older brothers. Being the last born, my mum doted on me. Spoilt me a little, I guess you could say. There's a six year difference between me and my oldest brother. I reckon there must have been a deep-seated jealousy harboured in him. First sons often have a special connection with their mums. Me coming along and taking away the attention from my older brother can't have been welcomed. That's what I've read anyway. I also read somewhere that mothers switch on a gay gene in their womb when having a third son. This is an evolutionary design to help ensure there was no sibling rivalry. In case two brothers fancied the same girl or something. The new gay addition to the family ensured a stronger bond within the family. Gays apparently have a higher emotional intelligence, generally speaking of course. Well, I'm afraid this evolutionary design backfired with our family.

My older brother sexually molested me from the ages of 12 to 16. There was always shame around the whole thing. In some way, I felt it was my fault I was being raped. When I turned 11 our dad had walked out on all of us. It was a rainy day in a suburb in Manchester. My oldest brother must have somehow felt it was all my fault. Perhaps I also took the attention of my mum from our dad. For some reason, I remember the pitter patter of rain on the roof of our three bed council house. It always seemed to rain in Manchester, especially on weekends. The sound of my mum weeping and the rain hitting the roof and window panes echoes in my memory even now. I reckon it was the sequence of events that made my oldest brother start to behave the way he did. I'm not entirely sure. I do know that for a long time all of us were terribly unhappy. I guess my older brother used me to relieve himself. In all senses of the word.

I decided to come out to my family when I turned 18. This was very hard. More so because of what my brother and I did. I was confused and ashamed of my sexuality. Nonetheless, I felt it was the right thing to do. Turns out I was wrong. My mum disowned me. This hurt more, because I thought I could do no wrong by my mum. My older brother stirred things up even more. I guess he thought he couldn't afford to have his secrets come out. Also it was his chance to rekindle his connection with my mum. My mum acted so cold. Not what I was used to. I felt like screaming from the top of my lungs. My own brother had raped me for years! But I chose not to. No good would come out of that. I would just be acting on my bitterness. I was predestined genetically to bring the family together, remember. Yes, this had backfired, but there was no reason to go out on a limb and shatter the family into smithereens. See what I did there with the surname? Good pun huh?

Anyway...I moved out and went to live in Birmingham. I managed to find myself a bedsit and a job. I worked and partied. I was lucky I had the ability to make friends easily. I could play the clown and was good at making people laugh. People were drawn to me because of my openness. I loved the attention, but underneath the excitement of socialising, there was always a deep-seated anxiety. What if my friends found out I was tainted by incestuous molestation? What if they knew the shame I harboured? I escaped into crazy parties and drugs, albeit always sensibly. Never over doing it. It made sense to me that you must have some respect for mind altering chemicals. I used to always wonder at some clubbers — popping ecstasy pills like they were eating smarties, then gurning like deranged lunatics in the middle of the dance floor.

I was mostly okay when I was with friends and partying, but when I returned home, I would be overcome with a deep sadness and loneliness. It felt crippling at times. But somehow there was a dissociation between it being real or authentic. I had this confident air about me. All my friends saw this, not the sadness I carried. For a time I coped with this lifestyle. Then things became dire after about two years. One early morning when walking back home from a club, I met a black guy called Dean. At least that's what he told me he was called. I met him on the street. I was drunk and he was helpful and charming. I later found out from his mum that he wasn't called Dean. He had a French name. He originated from a Jamaican town colonised by the French. But I'll come to that in due course.

I was taken in by his charm. In less than two weeks he convinced me to move in with him. I did, and soon realised he was a psychopath. He must have 'smelt' the deep-seated vulnerable victim in me. You see, psychopaths can sense 'vulnerable victim' even from your walk. I must have completely given it away when I walked home drunk on that cursed evening. He was all controlling and in no time was physically assaulting me. When family or friends came round, he would lock me in a cupboard underneath the stairs. He was not openly gay and I guess he felt ashamed of it. He would fuck me when he wanted. It was rape. He would then leave the room, with what appeared like shame protruding from each step he took. Perhaps that was just my imposed perception. I'd be left to clean up the mess. There was often a lot of sperm, which he sprayed everywhere. I was basically his sex toy and cleaner. For at least half a day after his ejaculation, he'd be nice as pie. Like a different person. It's like his anger was contained in his sperm. I'd always oblige on some level for sex, knowing that he was going to be chilled out afterwards. The more he came, the longer the grace I had.

He took me into work and picked me up at the end of the day. There was no window for me to even consider escaping. He had threatened that if I ever left he would find me and slit my throat. I believed him. Why use the words 'slit your throat?' It was too specific. If he had said 'kill me,' I may have believed him less.

Notwithstanding, I did manage to get away after about nine months. But after a few days, I got back in touch with him. I guess once you've been abused, the cells in your body become used to it. The cells crave for more as it's what they know. I phoned him and he picked me up.

When we got back, he fucked me straight away, coming like a fountain afterwards. As we lay recovering from sex, he decided to look through my phone. He was pleased I hadn't changed my password. I could see it in his smile. His satisfied controlling smile. He typed it in and looked at my messages, still smiling. This time I noticed a subtle difference. He turned around to look at me, and still smiling, he punched me straight in the face. I felt and heard something crack. I had no idea why he had decided to do this, albeit there never was a valid reason. He punched me again, this time in the neck. I leapt out of bed as blood was pouring out of my nose. He was precious about his white sheets. Blood stains on the bedding would possibly get me the death sentence. He got up as well, following me into the bathroom. All he kept saying was did I think he was stupid, as he brandished my phone in his hand. Till this day I have no idea what had triggered the violence. He'd ejaculated so much. Was his anger not coming out in his sperm any more? He proceeded to kick me in the stomach and I crumpled to the floor. This was the worst of the beatings I'd received in all the nine months since residing at his. Normally it was a punch or a slap and that would be it. This time he kept laying into me. He kicked me again in the stomach as I lay in a foetal position on the floor. He was just about to stomp on my head, when the doorbell went.

He rushed to the hallway. He must have recognised the silhouette of his mum through the opaque glass paned door, and came rushing back to me. I was still lying wretched on the bathroom floor. He pulled me by the arm and told me to be quiet. I knew the normal routine. I would be hurled into the cupboard under the stairs and told to be quiet. He didn't even have to gag and tape me up any more. Amazing what conditioning can do to you.

He shut the door behind me and went to welcome his mum in. I'd never met his mum before. He called her mum. She called him Edouard. Why was I surprised? Of course he had a fake name. I heard them walk into the living room and close the door behind them. I cried and prayed and then fell asleep. My brain's way of coping with the trauma I guessed.

I remember waking up to the sound of his mum's voice. She was talking really loudly on the phone. She was leaving the bathroom. She was getting ready to leave. There were always clothes in the cupboard. Mostly ones put out to give away to charity. I know...it doesn't make sense. A charitable psychopath. But life often doesn't make sense. I selected a mismatch of clothes, grateful for a pair of trainers that belonged to Edouard, but fit me. For some reason I decided to try and make a run for it. I was really afraid that this time he was going to kill me. I had to get away. He had never continued beating me the way he was doing.

I took a few deep breaths as I watched his mum through a crack in the door. She sauntered to the main door. Edouard wasn't with her. He shouted goodbye from the kitchen. I could hear him opening the fridge. This was my chance. No coming back this time, I promised myself. I opened the cupboard door and rushed towards the front door, just as Edouard's mum was opening it. Edouard was somehow now in the hallway. He spotted me and sprinted towards me. He was a tall, solidly built guy. His strong legs got him to me in no time. I only just made it to the door.

Edouard's mum screamed, perplexed as to what was going on. Edouard grabbed me by my shirt collar and pulled me backwards. The sheer force made me buckle and I fell backwards. His mum shouted some more, shouting at her son to tell her what's going on. *Your son is a psychopath and is trying to kill me* — I heard my mind say as I fell backwards, landing on my coccyx bone. It sent a shooting pain up my spine. I screamed for her to help me. His mum shut the door behind her and left. I lay there confused, wondering why she would just leave after she had just witnessed what she had. Denial I guess. Didn't want to believe her son was capable of such violence. Edouard dragged me on the floor by my arm. I shouted at him to do his worst. And he did. He beat me black and blue. There were bruises all over my body. He later raped me and left me in the room tied up and went to watch tv.

The next morning he drove me to work. Same time, like nothing had happened. I ached all over. My body felt like it had been run over by a truck, and then shoved into an industrial tumble drier. I felt sick. I could only breathe from one nostril. The other was blocked by congealed blood. He dropped me off and mentioned (again — like nothing had happened), he'll be there later to pick me up. I drifted into the office building where I worked. It was a car sales firm. In the open office, the fluorescent lights hurt my eyes. I went to the toilet and entered the first toilet cubicle. I'd never felt so grief stricken in all my life. I was the embodiment of quail egg shells and was about to shatter further. I sat down on the toilet and sobbed like an abandoned toddler. After feeling sufficiently numb, I left the toilet and went to sit at my desk. I tried to do some work but couldn't. I decided to go speak with my manager. I knocked and entered her office. I said I needed to speak to her. And before she had prepared herself. I informed her that the guy I'm with was going to kill me. I showed her my cuts and bruises all over my body, and pleaded for some time off so I could go back to the house, grab all my belongings and leave. She told me she wasn't sure she could give me leave as I'd used up all my holiday. I wondered whether she thought my cuts and bruises were fake. I told her again...enunciating each word. He's going to kill me. She again said she was really sorry. I went back to the toilet cubicle to cry. *No one cares that I'm going to be killed.* I eventually came out of the cubicle and my manager's manager spotted me and asked what was wrong. I guessed my disquietude had not been banished in the slightest by my tears. I said nothing and she insisted that I told her as she could see something was wrong. I told her and she was furious with my manager and told me she would deal with her. She got me a car and a driver and told me to go do what I need to do. *Life saver,* I thought to myself. Thank God for the power of reasoning.

I arrived at the house, every minute seemed like an hour. I used my key and quickly collected all my belongings. Yeah...I know what you're thinking. I had a key? Perhaps, it was a demonstration of his power and control over me? I had a key and still could not leave.

I checked each room, including the cupboard under the stairs. Memories came flashing back to me. The number of times I'd been kept prisoner in that cupboard. Why had it taken me a whole nine months for me to get my act together? Why had I decided I only deserved to be abused, raped and beaten? I guess I told myself that's what I was worth since my brother molested me at an early age. Well not anymore.

I was certain I had everything. I heard Edouard's voice, but soon realised it was my mind playing tricks on me. Echoey remnants of terror, left in my neurone network. I left the house and entered the car that had been kindly offered to chauffeur me wherever I felt safe.

I decided to go back home. My mum had missed me and she accepted me back. My older brother had moved, married and had a kid. Edouard phoned and texted relentlessly. After a few days, I decided to answer. A torrent of threats came through the phone. The same ones. I'm going to kill you if you don't come back. I told him to kill me already. That I had grown tired of the threats. I told him I was never coming back. There was no emotion as such, just clarity. He went mad. I listened to his crazed breathing down the phone for a bit before hanging up. He hasn't called again and he hasn't found me yet.

I found my own place and settled in. I'm scared to go out though. Afraid Edouard may see me, even though we're counties apart. He has a hold on me. I'd like to say not anymore. But I cannot bring myself to leave the house. I think I'm afraid of being out in the open. As if I didn't trust who else I could or would let in to my life to manipulate and own me like a puppet. I started therapy. Long overdue. Best thing I embarked upon, it allowed me to own my shame with sibling molestation and move past it. It wasn't my fault. I was young and my brother was young. We were all going through trauma. Our dad walked out on us. It affected us differently. The end. No need to over analyse it. It was actually really easy to let it all go once I was able to look at it from different perspectives. The problem is when you're in the thick of it. It's often next to impossible to look at anything from a different angle, other than your self-absorbed emotional barometer.

In that state, I had tried to kill myself once. I was about to hurl myself in front of a train and was pulled back by a passer-by. Selfish to the extreme. Disrupting a train journey. Possibly causing intense trauma for the train driver, and the cleaners that would have to clean up my brains from the railway tracks afterwards. But that's the state you wallow in if you're not able to come out of yourself and look at situations from different perspectives. Something I'm extremely grateful for having learnt to do whilst attending my therapy sessions. Subjects like mindfulness and basic meditation skills are being taught in schools now, about time I say.

So here I am, trapped in doors by my fear. My sex life is non-existent. Thank god for porn. I masturbate now and again. I sometimes wish my sex drive wasn't high. I sometimes admire people that don't have a sex drive. They must be peaceful in themselves. I try not to use porn all the time. Afraid I might be getting addicted, even though I'd say I wasn't an addictive personality. I'd say we all have addictions. Being addicted to abuse was mine. Fucked up huh? We can all be conditioned. Look at our relationship with TV and mobile phones. Healthy? I don't think so.

We need what we need based on what's familiar, until we somehow make peace with our longings and find alternatives. Determination and commitment — I'd like to say I tapped into this...eventually. I had to leave my past behind. I had to envision something else for me. I had to step out of victimhood. And the way I discovered it was to embrace my past and make peace with it. Yes, my brother fucked me... again and again. But I forgive him...He was troubled and in a dark place. We all were. He has to live with what he did to me. That must be pretty rough for him, so what good would it do me to hate him...or Edouard for that matter? Zilch. I had to make the best of my life.

You know what...Do you mind if we continue this outside in the garden? I'd really like to feel the sun on my face and just look how lovely that weather is...Hey, what if by narrating all this stuff I've finally shifted the fear? I know for a fact I really want to get out into that garden. Hope you don't mind. I'd really like to continue this outside. May have trouble with the reflection, but let's see eh.

## BDSM

Well, fuck me, would you prefer rescheduling this for another time? I just need a few minutes to vent. I'll be calm in a bit...I just get so sick of judging arseholes! I had a message from a recent sexual encounter who said they'd tested positive for syphilis. All I needed was a blood test. But of course, they have to ask their stupid questions. Yes, I had unprotected sex. I'm a grown adult and I wanted a raw dick up my arse! Can I just get the blood test now? I'm done with the disapproving judging glances you get from those nurses at the sexual clinic. Most of them could do with a raw dick up their arse to help them chill the fuck out. Honestly! Anyway...sorry. I'm all yours. You happy with this lighting and font? Okay...fine. Fire away.

My name is Caden O'Toole. I know, I know...sounds like a fucking porn stage name. Even funnier if I tell you I picked the name myself. I used to be a woman, believe it or not. Yep, that's right. I used to be a fucking woman with tits and everything. Had great tits too; I miss them...a little. Don't miss having a fanny though. Being a girl at birth softened my features as a bloke, I reckon. I have quite a round face, stubble and quite a broad nose for a white guy. My eyes are wood-brown and quite intense I'd say. A tough life is mirrored in them. I'd say I was a warrior in past lives. I'm quite an angry chap and if you hadn't already noticed I fucking swear a lot. I'll try to tone it down though. Can see from your facial expressions you're not best pleased with the language. Don't worry, I'll do my fucking best. Ha. Kidding. Not about me toning it down — just about swearing then. Never mind. Anyway...don't let my soft facial features deceive you. My eyes, I guess, are the one thing that may alert you to the fact that I'm a time bomb waiting to go off. I might tell you about my transition if we have time.

For now — you're more interested in my bondage slash masochism fetish right? Before I continue, I should tell you I'm also bisexual.

My transition may have some bearing on this fetish of mine actually, come to think of it. We'll see. Grab a drink and I'll try to tell you just how fucked up I am. Ha! Last time, I promise.

I think I like inflicting pain and receiving pain in equal measure. Not sure if that's the norm. I think some people are either masochists or sadists. Probably rare to be equally interested in both. But there you go. I'm certainly not normal. Love cock and ball bondage — I watched how to do that on YouTube. I particularly like that one being done to me. I did have concerns though at first. You know — as my cock was reconstructed. I soon found out I had nothing whatsoever to be worried about. It couldn't be pulled off or anything. The penis reconstruction is called phalloplasty. Not a delightful experience. For starters, I have a massive scar on my forearm from the skin graft used to construct my dick. The procedure's correct term is known as a radial forearm free flap (RFF) phalloplasty. I have a button in my right testicle which I press and hold to give me an erection. It's a pump, basically. Then when I've finished my business, I have another button, just back of my right testicle which I press just once to put my cock in the flaccid state again. I can't produce sperm as that requires testes and a prostate. Medical science draws the line at producing the external male genital. I never ever wanted kids. So that didn't bother me at all. Felt I was just too angry to have children. No desire to produce mini versions of me at all.

My balls are quite small, but still hang and have stretchy skin. Real looking enough. Did you know the constructed penis takes just over a year to heal and is quite macabre looking before all healed and ready to use? Hasten to say it's not something anyone chooses to do lightly. You have to really want to change your sex to do it. It's undoubtedly a desperate situation. Most people are prepared to do whatever. Can you imagine being trapped in the wrong body? Having the wrong sex organ? Most people can't.

Anyway, so much for — "will possibly tell you about my transition." Told you the whole damn thing. Though the mental preparation was another one to accomplish. The procedures are long and take their toll. I can tell you something. Once you've been through your transition, not much else life could throw at you that would make you even blink. So a word of advice. Don't mess with a transexual.

So back to BDSM. I love inflicting pain, mostly on men. When I want pain inflicted on me, I tend to go for the women. Is it some kind of subconscious thing to have women punish me for having changed my vagina to a penis? I don't think so. It's not necessarily normal. I think most gay guys would prefer men inflicting the pain. But then I'm not gay, I'm bi so that's that instantly resolved. Ha.

I definitely love humiliating and flogging men. That's a massive turn on. Tying men up and hanging them up from their ankles is a fine art. I had to go for training for that one. Paid fuc...sorry paid £200 for a week's training on that one. Had to really. I didn't want to cut the blood supply to someone hanging from the ceiling. All just to give me a hard on. Sorry, can't really use that phrase in my case, I just have to press a pump. Ha.

Being into BDSM calms me really. I know that sounds strange but it's true. I've always been an angry child. I have all this energy inside me. If I stay still, I can feel it bubbling inside me. Like a volcano about to erupt. I could never meditate. It's too much to be with really. One of my crazy hippie friends once told me that my body was home to more than one soul. I harboured several souls basically, all conflicting energies in my body. Crazy hippie arse! Sorry, that is a swear word, right?

I should say, for those of you out there making judgement — not that I care, because I assure you I don't — BDSM is not unnatural in the world. You only have to look at ducks fucking in a lake. The male pounces on the back of the female and uses his beak to put her into submission by biting on her neck — plunging her head into the water. If you have ever watched ducks fuck, it does not look pleasant for the female. It most definitely looks like torture. And just to ensure feminists aren't enraged by this — Female spiders and praying mantis' take this to another level with sexual cannibalism. I know that we are not ducks, spiders or mantis' but biological evolution 'threads' through us all. I don't care what anyone says.

I was brought up in a little town in Lincolnshire. There're three of us altogether. Me and two older sisters. I had an older brother before me who died at birth. This made my mum depressed for a while. My dad as well actually, I guess they thought it was their last chance of having a son. Little did they know. I felt like telling them, "Listen parents, I'm your son really. I just have the wrong sex organ." Their depression lasted about a year. Then after that I think they were just angry. My mum more so than my dad. Maybe it's just Lincolnshire. Apparently, the worst road rages in the UK occur in Lincoln. So — must be something in the water. Ha.

I'd say we were okay as a family. We didn't really want for anything. Cannot ask for more than that as a family. Don't get me wrong, we were just as dysfunctional as the next family. I remember my dad used to sulk something crazy which would wind my mum up no end. And it would just go on and on for weeks until they had sex. I used to hear them at it. Their room was right next to mine. They'd both moan so loud, you'd think two wild boars were mating. Yes, my parents could fit that description. After that they'd be right as rain. *Right as rain — Where did that phrase come from do you think? Most likely a farmer. A British farmer —* Anyway, my parents would be all smiling and courteous and affectionate to each other again. Why they didn't just fuck sooner always baffled me. But then again, I guess it doesn't work like that.

Both my sisters used to wonder why I didn't play with girl toys when I was growing up. My mum and dad just put it down to me being a tomboy. I think it somehow consoled them, now I look back. It comforted them somewhat that I was acting more like a boy than a girl.

My mum bought me a doll when I was eight years old. The next day I put it in the bin. They never bought me a doll after that. I played with toy trucks and cars and used to love playing football outside. I didn't even like wearing dresses. I used to always wear jeans and a t-shirt. I felt so different from other girls, that I became quite introverted. As I became a teenager, I got into Playstation and would often be online playing games. That was the one way I socialised. As an electronic shadow of myself. My profile was of a Japanese manga boy and no one questioned it. It was the one way I could discuss and interact, pretending I was a boy without making it plain obvious. When I wasn't on Playstation, I was building miniature electric vehicles. I was kind of a petrol head, you could say. I was into cars in a big way, from an early age. Knew all about mechanics and went on to study it at school. Again, people rolled eyes and heads. But not many. We *are* in the 21st century after all.

At an early age I set up my own car servicing company. People thought I was a lesbian and I let them believe that. I loved being a mechanic or a grease lesbian as people liked calling me back in Lincolnshire. I have to say I was really good at my job. I had money rolling in and I helped support my parents who were now getting on a bit. My two sisters came to visit now and again. They both got on like a house on fire. I was the water in the hose to quench the fire. I didn't really get along with them. We were like chalk and cheese. After all, I was a boy in a girl's body. They just thought I was weird. Since my transition, we get along a lot better.

Like I said, I was a mega petrol head. My car mechanic business was doing well. I bought myself a Tesla Roadster, one of the best sports cars in the world. The lesbians in our little town had the proper hots for me. They made it very obvious. I wanted sex with them but felt weird as my body didn't belong. With the few sexual encounters I had, I mostly got turned on when lashing their arses. Both the boys and girls. Actually, mostly the men. They wanted me to. And I really got into whipping and flogging. To be honest I think it was like some kind of an escape to get me away from my body identification crisis. It worked for a while...the crazy sex I mean. But what really got my juices flowing was driving at mega speeds in my Tesla. I would find country roads I knew were quiet and really go hell for leather. Again, it was like an escape. The thought of changing my sex never really occurred to me till after the accident.

It was a foggy Sunday morning in early August. There had been a lot of rain. I was testing the acceleration of the Tesla on my favourite country road. A rabbit... a fucking rabbit ran into the road. It probably had myxomatosis. Was more likely getting its own back on humans for giving it the terrible blinding disease. Anyway...I slammed the brakes. Bad move. At that same moment, I let go of the pedal, realising it was a bad idea. It didn't make a difference. It was too late. The road was wet. My car spun around instantly and I lost control.

I woke up in hospital with both legs bandaged and hung up. Both my thigh bones were badly broken — otherwise known as the femur — which is the longest and strongest bone in your body. Statistically, they only ever get broken in motor vehicle collisions. So there you are. My left arm was also in a splint, and I remember the pain. Oh my god! The pain I felt. I can't even begin to explain. I can't possibly put it into words. Except that there were levels of pain. In the first few weeks it was sub-acute pain. Keyword — acute. I was in agony. Pain threshold is a funny thing. Why even wake up? Why not go straight back into unconsciousness? You would think. The pain just radiated up and down my body. I was certainly present to it you could say. I turned my head and found a button to press. I pressed it, praying someone would attend with pain killers, rather than have to go fetch them. I prayed hard. A nurse did turn up. It seemed like a long wait. It was likely less than a minute though. He did have pain killers with him. All I said was the word agony. I thought that was quite an apt, succinct word to communicate the pain I was in. He injected something into my drip and in seconds a cold glaze came over me. The pain instantly vanished, leaving a slight numbness in my body. The power of drugs, eh. Chemists are geniuses really. I lay there thanking every dead and possibly living god for the advancement in chemistry.

I was in hospital for weeks. I'd done a lot of damage to my body in the accident. I had given myself a bad concussion too. The doctors were more concerned with that and were monitoring me. But it was all repairable. The doctor said I was very lucky. I'd be able to walk once all the healing had been done. Most nights I found it difficult to sleep. I pleaded that they put me in a cubicle. I'd been in the ward for weeks and weeks. The noise and lighting disrupted my sleep. Eventually, the doctors instructed that they should put me in a quieter space. Good quality sleep was paramount to my healing, they stressed.

It was when I had the privacy that I noticed I was feeling quite horny. I started to masturbate. Partly, I did it to distract myself from the pain, but then the pain eventually became part of it. I somehow tuned into the pain. Can't beat em, join em kind of scenario I guess. It made the orgasms really intense. The first time I did it after weeks of not, I squirted everywhere. It was so intense. I had to bite into my pillow to prevent me from screaming in ecstasy. I remember then wishing I had a penis. I tugged on my unusually large clitoris, wishing and visualising it as a penis. It was during these masturbation sessions in hospital that it really became clear to me I wanted to change my sex. It was also during my time in hospital that I truly cemented the BDSM bug into my cerebral cortex. I was really into the pain. It gave me the most intense orgasms I'd ever experienced. After weeks of masturbating, with not much else to do, I guess I got hooked.

I was in hospital for a total of two months. I was crazed at this stage. The pain had now gone into the chronic phase. That is when the fracture and soft tissue had finished healing. Pain after healing. Imagine. I'm surprised I'm not addicted to painkillers. I think if it wasn't for the masturbating, maybe I would have been addicted. Often, I refused the painkillers. I needed the pain for my orgasms. The irony is, I became addicted to the pain instead. Masturbating without some form of pain just didn't do it for me after my spell in hospital. My body was conditioned. Two months is all it took for my body to be conditioned. I wonder if that's the time period for most conditioning to be done to the human body?

Anyway, I was glad to get out of hospital. I had some support from family. My dad was particularly kind and generous with his time. My rehabilitation took a few weeks. I continued to decline the painkillers at night for reasons I've already explained.

One gloomy rainy morning, I decided to go for the sex change. There was no going back, once I'd made the decision. Skip forward a year — after several GRS and Psyche consultations. GRS stands for Gender Reassignment Surgery by the way — for those of you not in the know. I felt the whole consultation business was a waste of time personally. I'd lived as a man for a long time. I'd already had my psyche evaluation. But you know...got to keep in line with the rules. Besides, there was some talk that my concussion may have had something to do with my decision to change my sex. I knew of course that it didn't.

I sold my business, making a really good profit. And I had enough money to have the whole op, and even some spare cash to figure out what I wanted to do with my new life as a man. Like I mentioned before, there are many procedures. Most people spread these out over many years. I was fortunate enough to do them all together. Well, except the last bit which you have to wait for about a year before it can be carried out. Pay attention and I'll tell you all of them. I wrote them all down somewhere. Where, where...Here we are.

A hysterectomy, removal of the uterus.
An oophorectomy to remove the ovaries.
A vaginectomy to remove the vagina. (They can partially remove the vagina — but what's the point?)
A phalloplasty to turn a flap of donor skin into a phallus. That's the cock.
A scrotectomy to turn the labia majora into a scrotum, either with or without testicular implants. I chose to have testicular implants. I

wanted my penis to be as real looking as possible. Like I said I was fortunate. Others make do.

The last three procedures are a urethroplasty to lengthen and hook up the urethra inside the new phallus. A glansplasty to sculpt the appearance of an uncircumcised tip. If you want an uncircumcised tip of course. And a penile implant to allow for erection. That's the pump. This is the one I had to wait a year to be inserted. This was to make sure I had complete feeling in my new penis. RFF the forearm graft was the best one for sensitivity. Others where the skin is removed from your thigh or stomach or back muscles underneath your arm — don't result in as good sensitivity. I wanted my dick to look real, but I also wanted to feel it.

My breasts I had some grief over when they were removed. The formation of my penis however...I was elated when that was constructed. It was painful, yes. But nowhere near as painful as having both my legs broken. It was as if the experience of the car accident prepared me for the sex operation. I obviously opted for a big penis. What's the point otherwise? If I'm going to get a reconstructed dick I'm hardly going to go for a chipolata!

After the main operation, which cost me around £20,800, it took a year and seven weeks in total before I recovered.

It took some getting used to. The penis I mean. Like everything else in life. But in no time, I was swinging it around, every chance I got. I appreciated my constructed dick. I played with the pumps hidden in my ball sack. Erection, flaccid — hard, soft. It was a joy. I had a tattoo of a lotus flower done on my arm where the skin was grafted. The lotus flower kind of looked like a vagina in the end. But I left it. Thought of it as a sign to commemorate my lost vagina.

It's funny now looking back, I reckon I'd wanted a penis since I was a toddler. I wanted to be a boy. I was a boy. I just wondered for a long time where my penis was. At the time of course, you never make sense of it. Young and innocent you see.

Anyway, the price was pain, and lots of it. I had to undergo a lot of pain to get my sexual organ. I don't suppose it's any surprise that I now like pain with my sex. I had endured a lot of pain with my accident and now with the sex change. Not that I'm saying everyone who goes through excruciating pain turns into a pain junkie. But I did. Que sera.

At first, to test my new willy out, I decided to pay an escort for sex. I contacted him and paid to fuck him. I wanted to see how well my penis worked and thought it made sense to experiment with an escort. They had to do what I asked. I was paying. No awkwardness. At least that was the plan.

I decided to get in touch with someone who I felt I could trust. Don't ask me how I knew that, I just did. I wanted to fuck him with me on top. This guy bluntly refused, saying he never lay on his back when being fucked. He said he generally did not have penetrative sex. I kept raising the price. I'd searched for over an hour. He was the one guy I thought I'd be comfortable trying out my new penis with. In the end I offered £500 for a 30 minute session. He thankfully caved in. Not sure how much I would have continued raising otherwise. When I got to him, I pressed my pump just before knocking on his door. I was armpit sweaty with nerves. Using a newly constructed cock for the first time would do that to you I guess. He did lie on his back, with a smile too. So it didn't look forced. I was happy with the performance. Afterwards, I asked if I could use his bathroom. Once in there, I deflated my penis, dressed, came out and left.

Obviously, I wasn't sexually satisfied, not that I can ejaculate anyway. But I did get some pleasure. However, there was no pain involved, so that plain vanilla sex would have done nothing for me. I just wanted to know what it would feel like to fuck with a penis. It was quite something. It was particularly hot watching the pleasure on the guy's face. Unless he was faking it of course, he is an escort after all. I hope he wasn't faking it. I do hope he genuinely enjoyed it.

For once I feel complete. I was never complete. Can you imagine not ever feeling complete? Well, that's what it was like for me. I think my anger issues curbed as a result too. I don't get as irate and vexed. I can actually stay still, and that volcano inside me, you know, the turbulent feeling, is definitely lessened. So I know I did the right thing. I was in the wrong body and now I'm not. I still enjoy controlled pain with sex, but I can also be more passionate than I've been before. I think the BDSM side of me may be shifting. All part of my evolving. Medical science had to be involved for my evolution. Nothing wrong with that right? And now to find a sub for a relationship.

# CLOSET CASE

Good afternoon…or morning, or whatever time of day it is where you are. My name is Sebastian. I live in Australia with my girlfriend who is originally from Ukraine. I'm French. We both met when I was out on a work's do back in London. I lived there for a few years before moving to Australia. I'm a director for a big food supply company. I worked hard to get to the top. Always stuck my head into work really. It was my go to when everything else in life was unbearable. Don't get me wrong. Life is often good. I go on ski trips with my brother who I'm close to. Do a lot of things with my girlfriend. She manages her own arts and crafts shop. We have both been trying for a child for the last two years. IVF. It cost us thousands. Talia wants a child really bad and it turns out something is wrong with my sperm.

I think I was cursed because of something I did many years ago. I had a best mate who I was very close to. This was when I lived in Buckingham, before moving to London. We were like brothers and friends rolled into one. I called him my soulmate, because I genuinely believed he was my soulmate. Who says soulmates have to be a sexual thing? A soulmate can most certainly be a friend. I should know, I had one. I walked out on him many years ago back in the UK. Till this day I regret it. I regret it mostly because I thought removing him from my life would curb the sexual longings I've been having for men. It didn't, and I ended up losing my best friend. Every year I think about trying to contact him. Eight years have come and gone. Still not had the balls to get in touch. I don't have his number, but I know if I mean to find him I could. Social Media does have it's benefits.

So every year comes and goes and I've still not contacted my lost friend. And to console myself I do the most sordid thing, which just makes me hate myself even more. I live this secret other life in the shadows. I've gotten so good at being a chameleon, it's now second nature. God, didn't think this would be so hard. Admitting this, even here is difficult. How can that be? Fuck!

I have sex with men in public toilets.

I don't think I've ever admitted that out loud to myself, never mind to someone else. Even though you're hidden in the ether so to speak. Still damn difficult. I hang around public toilets and I've somehow mastered the art of figuring out who's up for it. Sometimes we go somewhere else to have sex, but its always somewhere outside. Doing it indoors would make it too real. I just couldn't do it behind a closed door. That, I reserve for my girlfriend. I know…it must be so hard not to be judging me right now, but there you are. I guess I'm an awful terrible person.

Am I bisexual? Really… I don't think so. It's easy to have sex with a woman. I just have to get hard. I'm not being funny, but you shove your dick in anything warm and wet and a hard on will be achieved. I don't think men need that emotional connection to perform. At least I don't. That's why our reproductive organs hang outside our bodies. Detached you see. I definitely think I'm full on gay. A part of me hates to admit that. Even now. I've just never associated myself with being a gay man. I don't know why. I'm not sure why I find it so difficult. Sometimes it makes me angry that I'm this way. This is part of the reason I don't contact this lost friend of mine. His name is Peter by the way. Peter Montgomery. I don't think I've said his name out loud since walking out on him back in the UK. Even though I know it's completely ridiculous, I partly blame him for the predicament I'm in. Sometimes I wish I never met him. I wish I never moved into the neighbourhood where I met him. And then I instantly feel sad. It's such a complex mix of emotions. What we had WAS incredible. I honestly don't have that with my girlfriend. Not even close. The connection. The laughs. The ability to conjure up each other's repressed child and nurture them. It was so freeing — I've never had that with anyone since I left the UK.

I'll tell you about it. From the beginning. Let's go back to when I first met Peter. It was on an estate in a newly built up urban area in Buckingham. I had just moved into a girl's house as a lodger. Steph was in her early thirties, and she was running her own property investment business. I did have reservations at first. But there were other guys also living there. It was a four bedroomed house. I was unpacking. It was a pleasant afternoon. Sunshine with low humidity. The doorbell chimed. Steph opened the door.

Peter and Steph met each other when they worked together at a young offenders. They exchanged niceties. I met eyes with Peter in the living room. Steph introduced us. My first impression was his larger than life personality, will probably be a handful. We started to enquire about each other straight away. I could tell immediately he was quite blunt. I liked him instantly. The British were generally polite and well mannered, unlike the French. It was refreshing to meet someone that said it how it was, unapologetically. He invited me round to his for dinner, I accepted. He mentioned something about it being part of his community service. I didn't understand what he meant at the time, but I just nodded and smiled.

The next day I visited Peter's for dinner. He only lived around the corner. I could tell instantly he was a good cook. He was preparing a fish meal. I sat on a stool and listened and watched him effortlessly manoeuvre himself around the kitchen. It was somewhat hypnotising, watching him chop, slit and cut different food stuffs. I found his voice and accent calming and easy to listen to. He spoke clearly. I thought for a moment he was taking care of his pronunciation, because my first language was French. I later discovered that was genuinely how he spoke.

The meal was amazing. It was a succulent and very tender bass fillet, with grilled asparagus and quinoa. The quinoa was prepared with a little garlic, chopped vine tomatoes, and chives. He sprinkled some maggi sauce on it. He finished it off with a decent sized wedge of lemon on the side of the plate. We sat and ate on stools in the kitchen. I ate slowly, savouring every mouthful. It was a very tasty meal. Peter talked the most but I didn't mind. I found him fascinating to listen to. He occasionally asked about me and also listened with acute intensity. Afterwards, we retreated to the living room where we had dessert. The dessert was crushed ginger biscuits for a base. Lemon curd, mascarpone cheese and cream whipped and placed on top and sprinkled toasted almonds to finish it off. This too was scrumptious. Peter had prepared these beforehand and it was set and cool from being in the fridge. I was blown away by his cuisine. *Little did I know at the time that I'd be blown, in other ways too.* I worked in the food industry and was quite a foody. His meals were scrumptious! Very scrumptious! Assured access to my heart for sure.

As we sat and ate in the living room, he revealed to me he was gay and that he fancied me. I was taken aback by his forthrightness. It seemed to have taken another level. At the same time I found him refreshing and respected him for his openness. I asked if it would be a problem for us as I was straight and he said no immediately. I hugged him. Not just because I thought it would be the right thing to do, but because I wanted to. I instantly liked him. Deep down I actually was chuffed that he fancied me. Of course, I never told him that. That evening, the meal, the chat, the openness. It was the start of an amazing friendship.

I found out there was an outdoor swimming pool in the estate we both lived in and I invited him to come swimming with me. I think deep down I wanted to show off my body. I hate to admit it but I wanted to tease him. I knew I had a great body and he fancied me. My ego would be polished. I'm human, flawed and narcissistic. We just do the best we can. Sometimes I enjoyed my ego being polished. Don't we all?

We had the best times. I taught him how to play golf. Occasionally, I went with him to a local theatre. Bought him a kite once for one of his birthdays. We had the most fun trying to keep it from being shredded in a gale force wind — We cried with laughter. We had great philosophical conversations. Also enjoyed playing squash and chess with him. We were both so competitive. Some evenings we watched a mind-boggling film, one of his recommendations. Perhaps, he was trying to tell me something? I never knew. I really enjoyed his company and I often stayed over, it was easy, I would like to say I didn't lead him on but looking back now, maybe I did. I kissed his forehead a lot and we hugged. A lot. I saw him like a brother. I'm French. We kiss and hug a lot. I'm affectionate, what can I say?

A few years in, I started seeing this girl. She was an up and coming singer. I did like her, but I also liked my friend Peter. I didn't want to see less of him just because I was now seeing someone. She started getting jealous. She didn't understand the connection Peter and I had. I didn't like being smothered. Well, it's a tough one really. I kind of like being doted on, but not when it restricts me. Does that even make sense? I'm an enigma really. Do you ever just have a whole load of contradictions about yourself?

Anyway, it wasn't long before my girlfriend dumped me. I was visiting Peter for the weekend at the time. She called me to say it wasn't working. I was just leaving Peter's. I told him. He seemed upset. He told me he was sure it would be fine. I didn't tell him she was jealous. Didn't want to make him feel bad. But I'm sure he guessed that was the case anyway. For the next few weeks he was really sweet. Always sending me funny and philosophical texts. Not as one text. Funny texts separately. And philosophical texts separately. I doubt you can get a funny, philosophical text in one, but I might be wrong. There might be some rubbish ones about the tree in the wood being felled, and if you weren't there when it was chopped down, did it really fall down. Lame.

I worked a lot — I just kept busy. That was how I coped with such things. I didn't necessarily miss my ex, I just felt a failure for not having a successful relationship. I guess you could say it bruised my ego. After moping for a while, I got back in touch with Peter. I mean properly. We both planned a trip to America to stay with one of his friends in San Francisco. It was one of the best holidays I've been on. Peter had also secretly planned a trip to Vegas. It was amazing. Just phenomenal.

Vegas was super cool. The first night was out of this world. There were these shows put on for free, outside the front of the main hotels. They were spectacular, and even better, free. One of the shows was a battle between two ships. Acrobats, waterworks and fireworks on an epic scale.

It was also the night that set in motion a place we couldn't come back from. We got paralytic drunk and staggered back to our hotel room. We had one of those debates that made me love Peter. We just had this way of sparking each other's neurons. We discussed for hours — Finally, we had decided to leave the bar we were in and walk home. Peter almost walked into a lamp post which made me laugh out loud. Finally we got back, and in no time we were on my bed. I was showing him pictures I'd taken whilst we were out. We were reminiscing over the day. I'm not too sure how it happened. But he started sucking me off. I was horny. It didn't take me long. He swallowed. I hate to admit it, but the orgasm was quite intense.

In his normal blunt manner, he informed me my cum tasted vile. This made me laugh. I handed him a glass of water, which he gulped down. I asked if he was okay and he said yes. I told him it was due to happen at some stage. I told him I don't want it happening again though. He said okay. I kissed his forehead and he went to his bed and I remained in mine and we both went to sleep.

The next morning I woke up with a hangover. I decided to boost my energy though and be overly enthusiastic about our biking trip. We both got showered and dressed quickly and went down to have breakfast. We're both conscious I'm sure, that food will make us feel a lot better. We had double the amount of juice probably for one table. We needed it. We ate our breakfast in silence. I'm certain it's not because we felt awkward. We had no qualms sitting in silence.

Eventually, after waiting for the breakfast to settle, we decided to venture outside to our bikes. Now, it could be hot in some areas of France. But my lord it was never this hot — It was roasting! You could see shimmering heat waves rising from every object. It was as if everything was being microwaved. Peter looked at me with a concerned expression. Again, I motivated us along. I was always able to motivate Peter in situations like this. Now, looking back, I guess he was always obliging because he fancied me.

After about 40 minutes of cycling, made bearable from some light breeze, I suggested we pull up at a bar for a cold drink. We both had tomato juice and vodka to hair the dog. We talked about the expression and its origin and were fascinated by our findings.

I asked if he wished to talk about last night, conscious he's a bit subdued. I repeated that what happened was bound to have happened sooner or later. Our bond was so close, I said. I told him I didn't regret it and if it's at all possible I only felt closer to him. This made him smile and blush at the same time. I reaffirmed that I would not want it to happen again though and he said of course and that we were both drunk. In no time, we lost ourselves in a completely different subject matter.

The next day we hired a car and drove to the Grand Canyon. Peter said he had always wanted to visit the Grand Canyon and he was so pleased I was with him. It was a long drive and we swapped driving a couple of times. When we did eventually get there, it was out of this world. Grand was an understatement. After walking about in awe for about an hour, we sat on one of the cliff edges in silence and watched the sun set. An experience I would never forget. Felt like an age went by but yet there wasn't enough time. Before getting up to leave, we both took a picture of our dangling feet.

The following day, whilst we're in the airport waiting for our flight back to San Francisco, Peter is grouchy. He got like that when he was hungry. Like a child really. Can't bear being hungry. I always have something in my pockets for these occasions. I offered him an energy bar. He took it with an action that could only be likened to primal instinct. He smiled, which always pleases me. We had had an argument earlier. We don't normally. The few times we had an argument it had upset me to see him hurt and upset. I didn't like it one bit. So I was super happy that he had cheered up. On the plane, I was really tired. Peter was broader and taller. I was shorter and smaller. I needed to rest my head. It seemed the logical thing to do, to rest my head on his shoulder. All I did was look at him and he knew what I wanted, and of course obliged.

Back home we knuckled down into work and we didn't see each other for a few months. We texted occasionally. I missed him like crazy, so I invited myself up from London. I suggested we go to the community pool and then go for something to eat. It was a Wednesday. The pool was open till 10pm on a Wednesday, and it was often quiet. I suggested we got stoned. It would give us a good appetite for later I said. We buddied up in a small storage room where they kept the inflatables.

Getting stoned was a huge mistake. I should never have suggested it. Subconsciously, maybe I wanted to cause the following events to unfold. Perhaps, I even needed the events to unfold the way they did. I go through this in my head, over and over until I can't stand it anymore. That is when I often decide to go to the public toilets for some distraction.

I decided to go a few lengths whilst Peter sat and watched. I knew that Peter only swam because I enjoyed it. It was obvious he wasn't keen on swimming. You could tell from his technique. Eventually, I got out of the pool and dried myself. He looked at me whilst I manoeuvred the towel around myself. There was a look in his eyes I don't believe I'd seen before. But then again, I'd never seen him stoned before. I decided to go up to him to retrieve the joint, he'd obviously had too much. I threw myself on the bunch of inflatables, bursting one of them. I asked him to give me the joint. He nagged in his usual way, telling me to watch the ash on the inflatables. I always found his nagging endearing. I knew full well he did it out of genuine care for me. I lied back and took a long drag. As I started to exhale, I felt fingers on my groin. I immediately asked what he was doing and no longer had I finished the question, my dick was in his mouth. His mouth was good. I'd actually missed his mouth. He did suck a good dick. Nonetheless, I was mad at him. Even though I was deriving pleasure — I was livid. I had stressed the point very clearly...I thought. I did not want this happening again. I had said that...twice. Yet here we were, my hard dick in his mouth. Why couldn't I just pull it out though? I didn't want to — It felt so good.

I got up. Shut the door. Turned him around and fucked him right there on the inflatables. I was so horny. I was also so angry. I fucked him hard. I wanted him to feel pain. I fucked him with all my might. Another one of the inflatables burst. I felt like pounding him through the inflatables into the concrete floor. It was intense animal sex. I'd never experienced that before. Again I didn't last long. I came in him. Pulling out to ejaculate didn't even come up as an option. I later found out it was called seeding — I seeded him. To my horror, when I pulled out, my dick was covered in shit. This only fuelled my anger. Peter lay on the inflatables writhing and masturbating. It was like he was possessed. He was most certainly out of control. I tried to wipe my soiled cock which was a little easy as it was still hard. I could easily have continued fucking him — Instead I decided to piss on him.

As I pissed on him, Peter ejaculated. Honestly, I had never witnessed anyone be engulfed in so much pleasure. I certainly had never caused any girl to convulse, writhe and moan the way Peter had. You would have thought I was exorcising him with my piss. And to think I had shoved my cock in a place supposedly not created for it. How could that be? How could I have put my dick in a place not made for it, yet caused so much pleasure? Perhaps there was something to be said about the male Gräfenberg spot after all — G-spot for short. Although for men, this is referred to as the P-spot — P for Prostate. Ernst Gräfenberg may never have known his study on the womens urethra in orgasms somehow extended to men!

I thought he'd never stop shooting his load, and to think I caused that. Secretly, I fostered the fact I'd caused him that much pleasure, but was damned if I was going to admit that. He had betrayed me — Betrayed us. The least I could do before leaving though, was wait till I was sure he had squirted his last shot of semen. Besides, I'm sure it's beyond rude to walk out on someone before they'd finished ejaculating. And yes honestly — I was transfixed by the orgasm. When his secretions had finally subsided, I pulled up my swimming shorts and walked out the room.

The experience caused me a lot of turmoil. I didn't know what it meant. What did it say about me? All my life, I was convinced I was a typical straight man. Yet here I was having just fucked a lad, and enjoyed it. It was too much to get my head around. I focused on Peter having gone against his word. I nurtured my hate for him and that got me through.

Eventually I moved to Australia. I needed to get as far away from Peter and that experience as possible. Australia seemed like a worthwhile bet. I met a girl in London and we both moved to settle there. How stupid of me to think that moving away would leave the experience behind. There was no getting away from it. It  was imprinted in my neural cortex. I hadn't just had sex with some random guy. I had sex with a mate that I had considered a soul mate. We were so close. No relationship had come close to what we had. I had walked out on him after fucking him. Left him drenched in cum and piss on a mountain of inflatables. I can still see him writhing in pleasure. I had caused that. Then I left him. It must have done something to me because I now go to public toilets for sex. Sex with men. I'm always turned on like crazy and then afterwards I'd loathe myself. Not necessarily for having cheated on my girlfriend. Mostly for having had sex yet again with another bloke. I'd always piss on them at the end. This was now like my signature.

Once, I noticed graffiti on a wall in one of the cubicles. Scribbled in block letters with a black pen were the words. 'Pisser please have me.' Underneath that was a mobile number. In another section it read. 'Anyone had the pisser?' I was referred to as the pisser. They were enquiring between themselves if they had been with the pisser. I guess it's funny.

I know this is fucked up. I'm not delusional about that. I should probably seek therapy. I want to believe I'm not gay. I just enjoy sex with men sometimes, is that even a thing? I must be deluding myself right? Bizarre situation. I honestly don't know what to do. Although, I'm convinced now more than ever that I need therapy. I most certainly should not be with my girlfriend. She deserves so much better.

I do think I should get back in touch with Peter. It's been years and nothing has shifted. I'm obviously affected by it. So might as well meet with him and at least have some form of closure? I really don't know. All I know is I can't carry on as I'm doing. In a way, I'm glad my girlfriend and I can't conceive. Secretly, I don't want us to have a child. It would just make things even more complicated, more permanent.

Informing you of this has definitely made me make my mind up. I'll break up with Talia. I'm sure it's the right thing to do. And I must get in contact with… I haven't even used his real name. That's how ashamed I am. It's not Peter. His real name is Ashley — That wasn't so hard. Ashley… God I miss him. I don't want to get with him or anything — I just need to see him. I just have to. Don't want to have to wait till I'm on my deathbed to get in touch.

## PODOPHILIA

Hi there, thanks for getting back in touch with me. I was hoping you would as I'm dying to share this with you — Sorry, I should start by introducing myself. My name is Logan. Logan Smith. I'm six feet tall, give or take half an inch. I truly believe on some days I gain the inch and others I lose it. I have one of those brick foreheads, you could say. Prominent forehead is probably a better, kinder way of describing it. I don't want you thinking I'm self-deprecating in any way. I'm not usually like that. Perhaps I'm a little nervous.

I have dark brown eyes with scanty eyebrows. A cute nose, if I say so myself and a mouth with a genetic propensity to smile rather than frown. If you know what I mean. I work a lot, I work for IT. You could say I'm a bit of a geek. I love role-playing games and I do enjoy playing epic adventures on Playstation. The company I work for is very good to their employees. We're trusted and hence not micromanaged. We're encouraged to question systems that we feel are flawed and are actually listened to. Can you imagine? Listened to and our comments acted upon. We also have a lot of rewards and incentives other than our salary which is pretty good. We have various forms of work stations. The standard desks, but also standing stations, beanbags, stools, lounge areas for meetings or one-to-one. The only thing left is a hammock put up from one end of a desk to another. That would be the ultimate chill out position for working on a laptop. I reckon we're not far off from putting the hammock up. So all in all there is no need to change job really. We're left to work from home when we want and we're allowed to make mistakes, as it's recognised that's where our learning lies. This is the environment we work in and so it's not surprising that we often want to do our very best. Why doesn't every other organisation do the same? That's always baffled me. Then again, humans baffle me and probably always will.

Anyway, I digress. The reason I wanted to do this, is to share with you something that happened to me a few years ago. Something that lead me into a different sex world. My sex drive has always been high. They do say that people with high sex drives are normally the ones that get into all sorts of weird shit. Not that I think what I'm into is that weird. If anything it's pretty basic as fetishes go. The other thing that people say leads people into some weird shit with sex is stress at work. Well, that's ruled out where I'm concerned as I've just mentioned the organisation I work for is one step away from being up there with the other best companies to work for like Facebook or Google or LinkedIn. See those examples, there's proof right there that geeks have all the fun!

I do think that my fetish was possibly brought on by something completely unrelated to sex. Apparently it can manifest like that. But I can't think of what that could have been. Perhaps as I go through this with you, it'll be revealed. Maybe not — I'm obviously delaying telling you what my fetish is. Isn't it weird how shame and sex related stuff is so entwined? Religion has a lot to answer for. I would argue that religion is the reason why there are so many fetishes. And trust me there are loads. Ones you can't even imagine. The list is actually endless. And I believe new ones keep coming up...every time.

I'm into feet, in a really big way. I started doing something with feet that was a bit way out there. But will tell you that later. I particularly love large masculine feet. Hairy too — Not like a hobbit's feet. That's going too far. Then again I won't be surprised if there's a whole new fetish around hobbit feet. People will be wearing hobbit feet slippers and getting turned on. If they're not already.

I love the smell of feet too. Not cheesy — The muskiness, or should I say funky smell of feet that have worked hard on a treadmill. Or just feet that have been cooped up in trainers all day. Peeling the socks off feet that have been active all day. Oh my god! Massive turn on. Firstly I'd get a good sniff — Then I would lick and suck the toes, putting two to three toes in my mouth at any one time, depending on the size of the feet. I think it goes without saying that it makes a difference if the toe nails are cut. Also no diseased toes or bunions in mouth, thank you very much. Although that again might be a thing for some people. I remember this one guy. I struggled to get his big toe in my mouth. It got me so turned on. The anticipation. How big would his dick be? Well, on that occasion I was disappointed. It was below average size. Just goes to show — The size of the feet don't always correlate with the size of the penis.

I love massaging feet. Have a lot of foot creams and scrubs. I can't understand people that don't like their feet being touched. It's such a relaxing thing to have done. But I guess, like anything. It's all on a spectrum. If there is a love for something on one end of the spectrum. There is bound to be a disgust for it on the other end.

I think my foot fetish started — or should I say — was incorporated into my neurone network at a very early age. Early teens. I was 12. Fancied this boy next door. I thought about him all the time. We used to wrestle on the floor. We would both get stiffies, but never acted on it. This went on for months and months.

Once when we were wrestling, he got his foot in my face. I got a whiff of that funky smell. And I licked his foot. He was taken aback at first, but then he just gave me the coyest look and smiled and we carried on wrestling. You know, it is not so much the feet, as the smell of the feet. The extreme of this smell is referred to as Bromodosis. And the whole smell thing, which of course transcends just feet, is called olfactophilia. The feet smell can be categorised into four main types — thanks to bacteria. Sweaty, cheesy, vinegary and cabbage-y. A combination of any of these turns me on no end.

Back to wrestling — A few weeks later, I went a bit further and sucked on Conrad's ring toe. That was the guy's name — Conrad. The ring toe is the one next to the little toe, or the pinky or baby toe. A few weeks later I sucked on Conrad's long toe. That's the toe next to the big toe. The big toe is otherwise known as the Hallux. That's when he moaned. At least I think he moaned, unless it was just my imagination. It is possible, when you're turned on, anything is possible. Things that disgust you just don't any more. I know I was young back then but I reckon I'd have stuck my tongue in his dirty arsehole. I fancied Conrad that much.

Don't get me wrong, we did other stuff other than wrestle on floors. Don't want you thinking that's all we got up to. Oh hello friend, where're we wrestling today? That's not how it was. My parents were often away and would leave the house to us. We could pick which floor we would like to wrestle in, carpeted was better. So all rooms other than the kitchen, bathroom and my parents' bedroom were okay. My parents trusted me. I wasn't an unruly kid growing up. You know...like some that pushed boundaries and so on. I was generally well behaved. I was an only child. Hanging out with my friend from next door was bliss. Otherwise, I reckon I'd have been quite lonely, having no siblings. Other than not having siblings my childhood was okay. No dramas. Parents were pretty normal. Perhaps too normal. Maybe we all need a little drama in our life. A little uncertainty is good for us. I remember reading that somewhere. Too much certainty wasn't good. It was all about the balance. Like everything else in life.

So I think it's clear where the foot fetish originated from. We don't need Freud to figure that out right? Fast forward then, to early 30's. I'm now just about to turn 40. I had to tread carefully, (excuse the pun), when it came to disclosing my feet fetish. Potential hookups could be so judgemental. It always amazed me just how judgemental people can be. I remember this one guy I had rimmed for at least 40 minutes. I then went to suck his toes and he jolted up in the bed and said that was gross. Calling me a perv straight away. He was blunt. Which I don't necessarily mind, it allows me to be the same. I followed his comment abruptly with - 'I just had my tongue play with a butt load of bacteria in your arse hole for close to an hour, yet you think sucking your toes is gross?' He stared at me like a gnome. I looked at him and looked at the door, then looked back at him. He didn't warrant any more words from me. I hoped that the glances made to the door and back at him were clear indications that he fuck off out of my flat. He got up, dressed sheepishly and left. I have no patience for people with no reasoning ability. I never have.

Don't get me wrong — people are entitled to what they like and what they don't like. But don't call me a pervert just because I like something you don't. What's that about?

Generally, most people are cool. I tend to tell people straight away about my fetish. I think it's best. It cuts through the crap. Then again sometimes, I choose not to divulge. I think on some level I decided to omit that part of my sexual desire. I figured, get to know someone and I'm sure they'll come round and eventually participate, because they'll want to join in so as to be with me. Perhaps I flatter myself. But someone has to.

In the early days, when I first started my foot fetish journey, people refused to hook up with me. Thought I was weird. This eventually made me stop revealing straight away about the fetish, like I mentioned earlier. But before I reviewed my morale on this, I decided to meet up with an escort. They would do what I want for money. I earned sufficient money for my work. I found this escort who had the most amazing feet. Large with tough black hair on the dorsum (that's the top of the foot leading from the ankle to the toes). This hair is called vellus hair. Normally it's very fine and fair. But this guy had coarse hair. Some on his toes too. Especially his hallux. (That's the large toe. Already told you that. You need to pay attention).

Like I said before, masculine, large, hairy feet with big toes really do it for me and this escort had it all. I think his name was AJ. He refused to give his real name. Fair enough, I thought, considering his profession. Now did you know that hairy feet is a sign of healthy feet? That's possibly why the attraction. Absence of hair on the feet usually meant there was poor circulation. So there you go. I'll give you time to check your feet. Cause I know you won't be able to help it. When you're done let me know, so I can continue.

Having this guy's feet at my disposal to do as I wish was proper hot. Luckily, he wasn't squeamish or ticklish. You might as well pour ice cold water on my dick when guys are like that. This guy just lay there and I licked and sniffed and sucked and stroked. Then I gave him a foot massage and used his feet to wank myself off. After which I sucked him off. I think he was pleased. And so was I. It was certainly £50 well spent.

I love feet so much I thought of changing careers to become a reflexologist. But then again, I may very well lose my license for molestation. Because, there'd definitely be no guarantee I wouldn't be turned on. Not sure it would be best practice, massaging a customer's feet with a raging hard on. So I had to scrap that plan almost as soon as I'd conjured up the idea. A bummer really. Would have been ideal.

Like I said, my sex drive is high. In time, sucking and licking toes started to become lame. Perhaps if I found someone to settle down with, I'd have kept my kinks tame. Who knows? I think when you're single and being promiscuous, it's like a permit to explore the boundaries even more. I guess it's never quite the same as having emotional sex with someone you love and so you're continually trying to get a better fix from the sex alone. That's what I think anyway. But finding a partner is not entirely in your control and after a while if you're actively searching, it becomes an act of desperation. No one ever fancies a desperate person. Neediness has never been sexy. So in the end, you end up chasing your tail. Ultimately, I decided to own or embrace my singledom and muster all my energy into being happy with what I did have. My freedom and my friends. What will be will be, was my mantra. If I was in a better headspace I was more likely to meet someone good for me. So that's the path I took. I put my foot into it. Ha! Alas, it led me into acts with feet that perhaps went to another level.

I met a guy after weeks of chatting on Grindr. For those of you who don't know, Grindr is a gay dating app. Really, its a gay shagging app, truth be told. Nothing wrong with that though. No judgement please. It is what it is. We had discovered that we had the same views on life. He loved his job and he made me laugh.

So this guy I'd been chatting with had mentioned fisting (that's where someone makes a fist and shoves it in your arse - with a lot of hardcore lubricant of course), and I had informed him straight away that I wasn't into that. I didn't want to hit 60 and become an adult baby, because I didn't have control of my sphincter muscle. So he hadn't mentioned it again. We decided to meet at a bar in town. This was verging on dating territory. Normally, hookups just met at home. Whoever was hosting.

When we met, he looked so much better in the flesh. I had never been good with sussing out if I'd fancy someone from looking at pictures. This guy was hot! I was delighted. More so as he thought I was hot too. We both complimented each other. I could tell from his eyes he meant it. I hoped my eyes portrayed the same.

His name was Aiden. He had short-cut light brown hair. Piercing blue eyes, akin to a cloudless summer sky. He had a defined jawline with stubble, kissable lips and broad shoulders. We didn't stay in the bar long. We just had the one drink and decided to leave. If society wasn't still infused with homophobia, we may have stayed and had a kiss in the bar. We could have felt comfortable touching and holding hands. But alas, there aren't many places in existence where gay men can do that without being worried some guy was going to bottle them. So we're forced to retreat back home. Where we can feel safe and allow ourselves to have romance. That's the reality for gay people still. Unless its a gay friendly area of town, like a bar in Soho, or on canal street in Manchester. So to all those that wonder why there's still need to have a Pride march or celebration. That's just one of the reasons.

We went to mine, and we were hardly through the door before our hands were all over each other. The chemistry was spot on. The kiss was electric. Tender and sensual and firm. His mouth tasted of mint and male pheromones and a hint of the cider he'd had at the bar. It was most assuredly a gourmet kiss. He pinned me to the wall and we snogged our faces off. Time froze. That's when you know you're engaged in a good kiss. After a while he pushed his hand down my jeans and found my arse. He put his finger on my bum hole and pressed against it hard. This made me quiver. He went from kissing my mouth to kissing my neck, then went up to my ear. He now had two fingers on my anus. He whispered into my ear. He wanted me. And he led me upstairs. In my own home. The confidence. I guess most bedrooms are upstairs. When we got to the top of the stairs, he opened his eyes for some direction. I pointed. And he again led the way, holding my hand. This was turning out to be very good indeed. I liked him instantaneously. Someone in charge, good-looking and confident and craving my arse.

We entered my bedroom and he nudged me onto the bed and carried on kissing me. He steered his hand into my jeans again and found my butt hole. He placed his fingers there again. And we embraced and kissed for ages. He was so sensual and forceful in equal measure. Perfect combination. He pushed one of his fingers into my arse hole slightly. Then took it out and smelled and tasted it. He made me taste it too. So erotic. ( I should say here that I had douched and showered — I'm not into brown.)

Eventually we peeled our clothes off. We did this slowly, smiling all the way. Even though instinctively, I think we both wanted to rip them off. I was pleased we were on the same page with delaying instant gratification. This fuelled the passion more. He then licked my feet and started to suck on my toes. I was elated. He sucked on his index finger and found my arse again and he continued to suck on my toes. I found the nearest bit of his flesh and sucked on that. It turned out to be his forearm. This guy ignited my whole body. I don't remember ever being so turned on by someone.

The foreplay went on for ages. I loved it. In the fullness of time, he opened his eyes and looked around my bedroom. He spotted the bottle of guava scented lube on the bedside table. He grabbed it and poured a lot on his fingers and then my butt hole. He proceeded to insert his fingers. He grabbed me and whilst smooching me, several fingers were going up there. Wasn't sure how many. I was enjoying that he was owning my arse. He knew how to put those fingers in. He had the knack. Some guys just ram them in, as if putting them up a lady that had had four or more children. There is a technique, and this guy knew it.

In due course, I was present to the stretch in my arse. I felt for his hand and he had all his fingers in and I hadn't noticed until then. I opened my eyes. He looked at me and whispered in my ear — let me. I asked if I'd see him again. If he was going to stretch my arse to this degree then I didn't want this to be a one off thing. He said he'd love to see me again.

Then with that said, he got up, put me on my back and raised my butt in the air. He lubed his toe, paying particular attention to his big toe. And he crouched over me and started to shove his hallux in my arse. He held onto my arse as he did this. Wanking me off at the same time. He got his large toe in with no problem. He had loosened me up. I was relaxed with him. That always helped. He looked into my eyes as he pushed his large toe and the toe next to it in. I squirmed. He somehow reached to kiss me. He was agile. It was the most erotic and sensual encounter I'd ever been in. I wanted all of him in me. How did I go from — 'No way am I being fisted to' — 'C'mon, put your leg in me already.'

Well that was that. When you fancy someone so much, you'd let them do anything to you. Perhaps some of you are saying speak for yourself, buddy. In which case, noted. I wanted this guy to do things to me I'd only briefly witnessed around corners of my cerebral cortex. I must have, somewhere in my psyche, had faith he would stick around when I became incontinent. Lol.

In the end, he had me crying with ecstatic pleasure. He had managed to get a good portion of his foot in my arse. He seemed to know just when to hold off, when to ease in and when to push it. Let's just say he was a genius at butt play and leave it there. My G-spot didn't know what had hit it. Like I said I was crying with pleasure. I couldn't believe my luck. And that's how the foot fetish went to another level. I had multiple orgasms. I'd only ever had that once before. I was orgasming and thought I was done and then it just continued. Not just women can have multiple orgasms you know. Get someone that knows what to do with your G-spot and you'll be doing the same. Guaranteed. I don't think only gay guys should be enjoying this. Straight guys should explore this too, in my opinion. I think you'll see less aggression in society, if more people enjoyed their butt being played with. Just my theory.

Anyhow, back to us. On reaching consummation, we lay there. The word spent is an understatement. We were both damp with sweat and panting a little. I liked his smell. I nestled into him like a child. I couldn't help myself. He cradled me, with no self consciousness on his part, whatsoever. I snuck up under his armpit and put my head on his chest. His smell was intoxicating. Pure muskiness. I wanted him again. How was that even possible? My arse was still throbbing. But I wanted him. I needed him to do something to my arse — Anything.

As if he'd read my mind, he turned around on his side, so we were in the 69 position. He put his semi hard cock in my mouth and he grabbed tissue from the side table. He wiped my butt of the excess lube and proceeded to eat my arse. And I mean eat it. Like his life depended on it. Like he was eating a juicy slice of melon on a hot muggy day. He stuck his tongue right up there. Sucking and licking my sore arse hole. It was so soothing. Such a turn on. He did this till I was beside myself with pleasure. I was gagging on his cock. deep-throating it the best I could. He was quite big. I have quite a sensitive gag reflex. But I didn't care. I wanted to please this guy. Fuck that I felt I was choking. I just took deep breaths and did my very best. That has to be love — suffocating so as to please someone. Now and then I got a taste of precum and I just lapped it up.

In perfect timing, he grabbed me, turned me around and slowly penetrated me. He fucked me slow and deep. Slow sensual thrusts whilst he wrapped me in his arms. He didn't stop kissing me till he ejaculated in my arse. He shook all over. I felt him squirt in my arse and that made me come. We both orgasmed together again, shuddering and moaning. He continued to kiss me. Slowly, passionately, tenderly. Then he stopped, and looked straight into my eyes and said — Of course I'll see you again. This made me smile. Then for some reason, I started crying. Why was I crying? Great, I was going to fuck up something before it had even started. He grabbed me and held me tight. He kissed my eyes, tasting my tears. Then he kissed my mouth, so I tasted my tears. I blurted out that I was sorry. I didn't know what was wrong with me and he said it was okay. He kissed me again, and said — Don't worry, I still want to see you, even though you're a blubbering mess. I'd like to get to know you. This made me smile and then laugh. We both laughed and cradled each other. We both took turns to look away from each other. But when either of us looked back at each other, we held our gaze on each other's eyes.

We didn't see each other for a few weeks after that. I think we both needed space to take in what had happened. At least that was the case for me. He texted now and then, to check up on me, and said he was thinking about me. Work was taking most of his time. But he said please not to worry. I trusted him. I don't know why. I just did. I had to, otherwise I'd have gone out of my mind. So honestly, I didn't have much of a choice. I kept busy. I didn't go on any of the apps. I had no desire to. Even if this didn't work, I was glad for the break. I put my head into games and carried on with a gaming project of my own which I was developing from scratch. This absorbed my time. As well as work of course. I also spent a lot of time with two close friends. I didn't have many friends. But the ones I had were quality.

So here I was. I'd decided to put myself into a very vulnerable situation. It does not get more vulnerable than having your arse stretched to the extreme. I'm sure the sphincter muscle is very resilient. I hoped it was, cause Aiden had put a spell on me and I was prepared to do anything with him. So there you go. Moral to the story. Never say never. You just don't know. I was more than happy to have a loose butt hole if it meant being with Aiden. It was a small price to pay, I thought.

A month and a half went by and I really began to think I wasn't going to see him again. I beat myself up for crying in his arms. How stupid of me. But then I consoled myself to the fact that I allowed my emotions to flow and there was nothing wrong with that. If he couldn't handle it then he wasn't the guy for me. I thought this — but I still felt sad. He had stopped texting a couple of weeks ago and I restrained myself from texting him. I had made it obvious that I liked him. If it wasn't meant to be then so be it. But I was damned if I was going to force it. I stuck my head into my gaming project more. And I defiantly stayed away from the dating apps. It would have been so easy to go back online to find the next shag. But I chose not to. My heart was breaking and I wanted to be present to it. I know, I know… you're thinking, surely not after one meet? It surprised me too. But there you go. Perhaps everyone's heart is not made of the same stuff. I wasn't going to question it, just be with it. I went for long walks. Visited the gym four times a week. A few more weeks went past. They all kinda rolled into one. I was grateful for the blurring of time. It meant I was getting over it. They do say, time eventually heals all.

One stormy evening. I was contemplating which movie to watch. It was the weekend. I made myself a cup of tea and started to scroll through Netflix. It was raining hard. Every now and then, there were flashes of lightning. I'd always loved storms. There was something exciting about it. This particular evening though I seemed to have a bit more excitement than usual. Right in the pit of my stomach. It was like the feeling you get when you know something great was going to happen. Do you ever get that? Surely it's not just me. This excitement was coupled with a good bout of contentment. I took a deep breath and smiled from ear to ear. I took a sip of my tea. Finally, I decided to watch a Swedish thriller with subtitles. I loved these. I didn't want to scroll and scroll for ages and ruin the contentment I was having. No sooner had I pressed enter on the remote control, then the doorbell went. I got up to answer the door, wondering who it could be and hoping he or she had an umbrella. I opened the door and there stood without an umbrella, was Aiden. He was soaked through, but still had a smile on his face.

## FURRIES

Hi there, I'm Donald. It's really nice to make your acquaintance. I'm 27 years old. Gosh, this is sounding all a bit formal isn't it? I've never been interviewed this way before, so please bear with me. I'm sure once I relax I'll be a lot more natural. I'm 6ft and 3in tall. I'm a little chubby with a bit of a tummy. Once when wearing a fairly tight t-shirt, a close friend of mine said my tummy looked like a large doughnut was concealed under my shirt. Who needs close friends huh? Guess it's not as bad as being told you look like you swallowed a teletubby. That was also a so-called friend. Even though my weight is above average, I'm quite light on my feet, also I'm quite nimble. Not sure I'm making sense but it's the best I can do to describe it. I guess you could call me a gentle giant. I have very blond light wispy hair which is often a nightmare to keep in place, especially in the wind. I have light brown eyes and almost no eyebrows. My eyes are quite large, which I guess matches my large head. For a big guy I tend not to perspire a lot, even after a long walk or some form of strenuous exercise. The most I get is damp. I'm quite pleased about this. There's nothing worse than dripping with sweat I think. Maybe that's why I don't lose weight easily. I don't sweat it off like most people can. That's what I tell myself anyway. Good an excuse as any for being a fatty I suppose.

Anyway, I'm a graphic designer by profession and love my job...most of the time. Until I have to deal with bureaucratic bullshit. Then I don't like it so much. I've worked for a company called 'Blueprint//Tag' now for about three years. As a hobby I love manga very much. You know...Japanese animation. I'm also heavily into role-playing games. I guess you could say I'm a typical geek. Maybe not so typical. I'll let you decide that when I tell you what I'm into. I love costume parties a lot. Which leads me onto what I'm here to tell you.

I recently found myself hooked on dressing up in furry animal costumes. I mean the full gear. I get a major kick out of it. There is a sexual thing to it. But it's more than that. I'll try to explain.

Like I said, I'd always been into role-playing games. Right from when I was a toddler really. I used to sit and play on the floor in the guest room to our house. My dad owned a large five bedroom house. We rarely had guests stay and so the guest room eventually turned into my play room. I had boxes of toys which I'd gradually moved into the room over the years. I would sit and build an entire city with roads put together like pieces of a large jigsaw puzzle. Then I would build Lego buildings. I remember having just as many petrol stations as houses. This was a good thing as I had a lot of toy cars. I would sit there for hours on my own, playing 'families'. I had an older sister, but we didn't get along. We both thought each other were weird. Our parents often left us to our own devices. Some would say it verged on neglect. But I think we were okay.

Both my sister and I were very mature for our age. We both effortlessly got straight A's at school. My sister got awarded a scholarship at a prestigious university and left home. My parents then gave me more attention. I guess they thought my sister and I got on, and now that she was gone they should make an effort. Guess you could say they both had poor observational skills. Nonetheless, I lapped up the attention, asking for more role-playing games and games for the PC. I mostly played games on my computer. My dad got me the most powerful drive for my computer, again perhaps to make up for the fact that he found it difficult to engage with me in any other way. There was always an awkwardness in the air with our family. I never quite understood it. It was as if there was a deep dark secret lurking in the ether. Every time my dad or mum mentioned they had to tell me something at the dinner table, my heart would skip a beat, and I'd brace myself for the worse. "Here we go, finally the elephant in the room is about to be revealed," I would think. But whatever they said was never a big deal. I'd be disappointed. Crazy huh? Disappointed that the news was not bad enough.

I loved the open world games. They were awesome. I was a fan of the final fantasy games. I loved all the characters. I remember starting to pretend I was some of the characters. That is perhaps when it all started.

I should probably tell you what furries actually are. Essentially, it's people dressed up in 'cartoony' animal costumes. Mostly white men in their mid twenties and thirties are into this...for now at least. I'm not too sure how I got into it, if I'm honest. Maybe it has something to do with my love of manga and role play. That's all I can think of. Perhaps wearing costumes hides me away from myself. I haven't got the greatest looking body. Never really thought about that. I can't remember looking in a mirror at myself. Even when I brushed my teeth in front of a mirror, I would close my eyes. Like seeing a reflection of myself would immediately turn me into the Candyman or something. I just never looked at myself. So perhaps that's why hiding in a costume was appealing. Kinda makes sense.

It took me a while to decide which costume I liked the most. In the end I decided to be a tiger. They are heavy but agile and light on their feet. Thought this was fitting. There is also something sexy about the tiger. Daring, wild and sexy. That's what I think anyway. So I visited two shops before choosing the right tiger costume. When I tried it on in my bedroom, I was beside myself with excitement. It was like I'd stepped into another world. Looking at myself in the mirror for perhaps the first time since being an adult, I can't describe what it felt like. I instantly got aroused. I thought to myself how cool it would be to be amongst other guys in costumes and be able to masturbate without anyone knowing. Random thought. But there you are. I decided to figure it out. So I made a slit where I could put my hand through the costume to my groin, whilst having it concealed by the tiger's paw, which was essentially a glove. I refined the costume with some velcro. This allowed me to attach my right paw to my waist, just next to where my hand disappears down my groin. I could then play with myself to my heart's content. It was ideal. No one knew. I'd stand and mingle whilst playing with my dingle for hours sometimes. Edging the whole time...

Say what? Oh what's edging... Edging is what you do when you get close to coming then stop yourself repeatedly. When you do finally let go, it's intense. And I could cum and moan in the middle of everyone and no one would be the wiser. I was hidden behind a mask. It was amazing. It didn't bother me that the inside of my costume would be covered in cum. I quite liked it. Besides, it dried quickly. I always wondered if everyone did the same. But I never asked. For one, it meant you had to come out of character and no one wanted to do that. Dressing in costumes was the whole point. In costume and character, we could stay hidden in our fantasy world. Another thing I came to realise, it didn't matter if there was any awkwardness, pain or sadness cues in our body language. It was all concealed in our costumes and we just stayed in character. This was especially great relief after dealing with the awkwardness with my family for so many years, and not ever knowing why it was so.

I loved attending the furries conventions. They held quite a few of them at both ends of the county. Of course, the first one I attended I was nervous as hell. But again it didn't matter because I was hidden behind my costume. If only people were allowed to give presentations wearing full-bodied costumes, even just face masks. I reckon people would be less scared of talking in public then.

The first convention I attended was where I met my man. He was the cutest jaguar you've ever seen. Dark inset eyes, cute as ever. Covered in dark velvety fur from top to bottom. He was the same height as me. I was drawn to his character straight away and I loved the traits he portrayed. When we first met, he picked up his tail and entangled it with mine. It was a nice gesture. I was flattered. He made an audible roar sound and I reciprocated. I was masturbating at the time, but I stopped. I felt like he could see me even through the mask and costume. He did actually put his paw next to my groin, looked down and then looked up. I think he guessed what I was doing, but I wasn't sure. Nonetheless, it made me conscious and I stopped. He held my paw and he led me to a balcony. There were several balconies. Four on each side of the ginormous ballroom we were in. It was an amazing ballroom belonging to a philanthropist. People knew who he was because he was often doing amazing things for charity. He had inherited a lot of money from his grandfather. It seemed only fair he gave some away.

The ballroom was as large as the one in the Walt Disney movie — Beauty and the Beast. It had a grand winding staircase with golden handrails. This was majestic and central to the room. The walls were covered in great big mirrors, all rimmed in gold. All of us could take delight in seeing how we looked and how we mingled with the other furries. An irony really, as I assumed like me, none of us enjoyed looking at ourselves otherwise. Like I said, an assumption on my part. The ceiling was a marble architecture quite unlike anything I'd ever seen. The floor was polished ironwood, the hardest wood in the world. All the way from Australia. The geek in me looked it up. Ironwood has a Janka hardness of 5,060 ibf. That's basically the force required to embed an 11.28mm steel ball into the wood half the ball's diameter. Larger force — harder wood. Ironwood required the most force.

The room was enchanting, just like I'd imagine the ballroom in Beauty and the Beast would be. We all strutted our furry butts with pride, not caring about a thing in the world. Again I know an assumption on my part. But we were all in character with whichever animal we had chosen. And I liked to think that *none* of us cared about a thing when we were in that ballroom being cartoon animals.

When my jaguar got me to the balcony, he proceeded to spell out his name, using his hands. I wasn't sure if it was something every furry did. But I had learnt sign language, so I could communicate if I needed to. He communicated that his name was Toby. I asked if that was his real name. And he signed —funny. And then signed — of course. I signed back that my name was Donald and it was a pleasure to meet him. He signed back — likewise. Then he took hold of my hand again and we stood and looked out at the view. It was the countryside. Breathtaking, undulating hills and woodland, and fields of yellow. It was rapeseed season and they were ripe for harvest. The air was filled with the scent of Sweet Alyssum. These were planted in large glazed blue terracotta pots; one situated on each end of the balcony. We stood and looked out into the countryside for ages. Like we had known each other forever. I could almost imagine what he looked like underneath the costume and I expected he did the same. The mind can imagine anything and make it real. I noticed some people arranging things further on in the distance, at the edge of one of the fields. I wondered what they were doing. I signed the question to Toby and he signed back that he didn't know.

The music suddenly stopped playing in the ballroom. It was epic orchestral music, most of which was from the Final Fantasy Games on PS4. An announcement was made. The party was being extended till late at night, and there was going to be a fireworks display as soon as it was dusk. That explained what the people were doing over the horizon. We could all congregate to watch the sunset and then in about 80 minutes, (which was roughly the time it took to get dark after sunset), the fireworks would be ignited. Did you know fireworks first originated in China about 2,000 years ago? The most popular story of origin, is that it was invented by accident when a cook created an explosion by mixing charcoal, Sulphur and saltpeter. The explosion happened after the mixture burned and then was compressed. Oh, and the Chinese believe fireworks can ward off evil spirits...Sorry the geek in me again.

Where was I? Oh Yea...so Toby signed to ask if I fancied staying and I signed back to say most definitely. Why on earth would I want this fantasy to end? In a majestic ballroom, in the middle of the countryside, holding hands with a cute jaguar. And now we were allowed to stay longer to watch the sunset and then fireworks. Why on earth would I want to leave? Toby nudged me with his head on my shoulder and cheek and I did the same. Cats in the wild do this to show affection and it's called bunting. I can't say we looked this up. It just came instinctively to us to do it. Then we took turns in placing our heads on each other's shoulders and continued to observe the colours of the sky and fields and woods whilst breathing in the Sweet Alyssum. The scent was somehow pleasantly infused with the smell of our costumes. It was what I'd always imagined heaven would be like.

That evening was just like I thought it would be — nothing short of spectacular. The sunset stripped away all of our egos by force, and left us standing there in awe, gawking at possibly one of nature's most beautiful wonders. We had about 80 minutes to soak up the atmosphere. Then the firework display commenced. The sparks and colours and patterns and bangs, were out of this world. I was willing to bet that all of our demons were exorcised as a result of the fireworks that evening. It was truly memorable. One I'd imagine I'll recall on my deathbed with a smile. It was phenomenal. Gives me goosebumps thinking about it now. Can you see? Look at my arm.

Anyway, after that breathtaking event. Toby and I started seeing each other. The first thing I noticed was his musky smell. He had sweated quite a bit in the costume. I hardly sweat remember, and I'd forgotten other people do. It made me wonder if sweat and smell was also a thing for furries, as in most cases this would be unavoidable. Except of course, if you had a shower straight after getting out of the costume. But that's not how it happened for Toby and me. I was thrilled to see what was revealed from the costume. Excited to see if my imagination was close or far out. I wanted him straight after taking the costume off. But of course this could be different for other people. For me when the chemistry is strong, the sweat smell becomes intoxicating and just adds to the attraction I reckon. Neither of us were Adonis gods, but we had formed a bond. And the chemistry was electric. We had probably absorbed some of the sparks from the fireworks display. We had great sex and we had no inhibitions with role-playing now and again, which just heightened our orgasms beyond measure.

We did continue to go to conventions, and we went to all of the ones staged and held by the millionaire in the countryside. Whilst this guy was wealthy he was very down to earth. He certainly wasn't your pick of the mill millionaires. He was very intellectually smart and had a great capacity to reason. He wasn't like the tagline of the advert for the Galaxy hot chocolate drink — He wasn't luxuriously thick! Like some others I know, whose names I won't mention. This is why it was a terrible shame when he passed away, five other spectacular conventions later. Everyone turned up to his final event. It was his after party, following his funeral. It took everyone's breath away, as expected. He was greatly admired and respected. Which was amusing in a way, because his costume was a rat!

In time, I left home and went to live with Toby who was 10 years older than me. He had a lovely home...also in the country and he got a puppy when I moved in. It felt like family straight away. I was mostly glad because there was none of the awkwardness which always hung around with my family. I settled in sooner than I thought I would. Toby and I soon established our roles within the house. Toby enjoys cleaning and DIY and I enjoy cooking and gardening.

One evening, it all came to light why I had that sinking feeling of awkwardness with my family that I couldn't explain. The phone rang. Toby and I had just had sex. I ran down the stairs naked to answer the call. It was my mum on the phone, she was crying. I asked her what was the matter and she couldn't speak. I had to wait for her to cry out. It took about 15 minutes. Eventually, she said my dad and her had split up. My heart sunk. Then she said, that wasn't the issue, as they hadn't been getting on for ages. She started to cry again. I had to wait another 15 minutes. Yup no kidding, another 15 minutes, I timed it. What she eventually came out with shook me to the very core. My legs gave way and I slumped to the floor. I forgot how to breathe.

As if Toby sensed something was wrong, he came running down the stairs, also naked. Watching his flaccid willy flop from side to side, brought me back to consciousness. I asked my mum to repeat what she had just told me, just in case I had misheard. It does happen. The brain hears things that were never said. She said it again. Yup...I was adopted.

Apparently both of them had agreed to adopt me when I was a baby. My birth mother died giving birth and I had no family. I was immediately put in care and then a foster home. But very soon afterwards my non biological parents came along. Now it made sense — all those times of awkwardness around them. I knew in my very core something was not right. And at one stage I thought I was losing my mind. Because they never said anything. Advice to parents out there. Tell your children whatever it is going on. Especially if it's impacting you emotionally — Cause a large bet is, your children will pick up on it. And to not tell them is to make them possibly go insane. Keeping family secrets never helped anyone, *ever*.

I was so grateful for Toby who sat with me on the cold tiled floor. My bum hole was constricting and contracting with the cold. And I suspect so was Toby's, but he just sat there with me whilst I cried into his shoulder. The fact that I'd always sensed something was wrong, softened the blow somewhat. I took some solace in that. It was like I was prepared. But I'm certain that having Toby with me was a massive help. I'm not sure what I would have done otherwise. We continued to sit there for another few minutes. Eventually we did get up. I reckon we were both close to getting piles if we hadn't moved our butts.

We went back upstairs and we both got into our costumes and lay on the bed and cuddled. Me as tiger and Toby as jaguar. Our puppy came in after us, he was called Teddy. He loved cuddling up to us when we were in costume. We lay there for a long time, my head in the crevice of Toby's chest and shoulder. My breathing eventually slowed down and I was calm. I was with my family. Even though I still felt my dad and mum were my parents, for a long time it hadn't been authentic. What Toby and I had was authentic. There was no question about it. I was content.

My sister was now not blood related. Our squabbles over the years now made sense. Nonetheless, we became a lot closer after that event. My mum and dad were amicable. I told my mum about my fetish. She already knew I was gay. She didn't really understand what I was telling her, so I had to explain quite slowly. Eventually, I think she just gave in. I don't think she understood it. She just accepted it. She met Toby and she liked him very much. That helped her accept the furry fetish. That and the fact she felt guilty for having not told me I was adopted all those years. I could have done anything, and she would have been okay with it.

It took awhile for her to stop apologising every other week or month. She had tried so many times to tell me, she said. All those times at the dining table, when I thought they were going to reveal something. Her apologising all the time was a pain. I had to give her a lecture about feeling guilty. Informed her if she didn't stop she was bound to give herself cancer. I had read that somewhere. Harbouring negative emotions was not good for our cells. She did eventually stop, when she realised I was totally fine. As far as I was concerned, she was my mum and my father was my dad. They had brought me up. It wasn't too difficult to reason that through. They were and will remain my parents.

I was glad the 'elephant in the room' was led to its grave finally. I was glad that I'd opened up to my mum about my fetish and was also glad that my sister and I had become closer since realising we weren't blood siblings. I was adopted, and yet I had created for myself the best family anyone could ever dream of. I'd always envisioned being in a close and loving family. That's what I had in my mind's eye all the time, when I sat down to play in the guest room on my own. When I was online playing games on my computer or when I was role-playing. I always saw myself as being in a loving, caring family and I suppose that's what had to come to pass, despite all odds.

CBT

Hey. How you all doing? Having a great day? Hope so, cause here in Germany it's a beautiful day. Ah… Hang on a second…

Sorry about that, my dog was whining. She's a Bichon Frise. She's two years old, so still a puppy. Still not great without attention. I have her on my lap now. It looks like she's been crying, but dogs don't cry. Although I'm sure a lot of people would want to believe they do. I'm hoping she doesn't have an allergy or even worse has blocked tear ducts. Then they can have a discharge from the eyes called epiphora. That would mean a vet bill. I could do without that right now. I just had to pay out for my car, boiler service *and* ventilation unit in the house. Does anyone ever wonder why it seems financial expenses all crop up at once? And often when you've decided to watch your pennies. Also misfortunes happening in three's, weird. Anyway…hopefully it's just a speck of dirt in her eye. I will continue.

My name is Caleb. I'm 5ft 10 inches. I guess you could say I have an athletic body. Don't like to brag. I try to exercise and eat well. I have light brown eyes, I'd say like polished oak. I have some kind of stubble. Can't quite grow a beard. I tried. It ends up looking patchy. Not a good look. I'd say I'm okay looking. I shouldn't make you nauseous if you looked at me, at least. And the final thing I should say is, I'm straight. I know, I know — you're wondering why the hell I'm on this forum then. Well, that has something to do with my kink. My fetish. The daring thing I'm into that I'm here to share. So please hear me out or read me out… whatever.

I'm into something some people call 'ball busting' and others know more technically as 'cock ball torture.' Otherwise shortened to CBT. This always makes me giggle cause the other use of the acronym for CBT is cognitive behavioural therapy. Arguably, this could be used to eradicate unwanted sexual interests or compulsion. CBT used to eradicate CBT. Funny huh? Well I think it is. Love funny ironies like that in life. I don't feel a need to eliminate my compulsion. So far as I'm safe, I really don't see a problem with it.

So where and how did I develop this fetish of mine — I hear you ask? I've been into ballbusting since I was 14 years old. Lol. Ballbusting...sounds nuts right? Ha — no pun intended. I don't feel anything led me towards this fetish. I feel I had a pretty normal childhood. Perhaps too normal. Maybe that was the problem. Who knows? I grew up in the lovely village of Ramsau. It's a very picturesque village, with a population of 1,800 people. Lots of people go there to see the Alps. The scenery is amazing. Post card amazing. The view of the Parish church of Sebastian in winter is just breathtaking. I know I'm biased. But it's true. The air is always fresh and subtly scented with some sweet smelling shrub or the other. They could easily create a real life film of the animated movie 'Frozen' in that village. Living here, I suppose you could say I'm exposed to people from all over the world as it's a tourist destination. So luckily, I don't have xenophobia. A real problem in society at present, it seems.

My parents met in an art class and became lovers very quickly, getting married just after a year of courting. I suppose you could say when you know — you just know. They were and still are very much in love. I was the oldest brother of three. I'm quite close to my brothers, although we don't see each other very much. One of my brothers moved to the United States with his girlfriend, who he met whilst travelling. And my other brother moved to London, also with a girlfriend he met whilst travelling....but in Africa. We definitely meet every year, for a family reunion. So it's not all that bad.

When growing up I was a bit of a live wire. Always seeking an adrenaline rush. Love extreme sports. Although I'm getting on now, so don't do as much. Still enjoy white water rafting and mountain biking. I also own a motorbike. I get a real buzz out of these activities — makes me feel alive. I guess we all have our thing that makes us feel the most alive right? Mine is daring sport, for sure. For some, it's perhaps connection or travelling.

Siblings and I all attended university and embarked on professions requiring the use of our brain. One of my brothers is a financial analyst. My other brother works for a scientific editorial company and I work for the local government as a parks ranger. I acquired a masters in Ecology and love being outside in nature. I also love driving my quad bike through the parks. All linking into my love for an adrenaline rush. None of us in my family are religious. I'd like to think we're all rational, liberal and open minded about things. We don't know how to be any other way.

Like I mentioned, I was first fascinated with my balls when I was 14 years old. I have quite big ones that hang quite low. And...I don't know, I used to grab and pull them when I was masturbating. I guess you could say I'm quite tactile. Once, when I was grabbing them and had them squeezed so tight the balls were pressed up against my scrotal sac, I decided to tap the underneath with a pen. It hurt a bit, but it was an interesting hurt. I felt the pain inside churn up into my stomach and it was a nice feeling. I mean, I only ever did it when I was aroused. It might be a different thing if I was flaccid, I'm sure. But lightly tapping on my balls when masturbating certainly intensified my orgasms. And it really just sprung from there. To be honest, I thought a lot of people did this, until I found out it wasn't the norm. Although, a lot more people are into it than you think. That's the thing with sex. It's all taboo and hush, hush. You never know what's going on in people's bedrooms.

Well, after a few sessions of pen tapping — of course I started to hit a bit harder. Until in time, I was grabbing my scrotal sac and hitting my balls on a table. I loved the intense feeling you got. The mix of pain and pleasure was immense. That's my experience anyway. Of course, I have since looked it up after finding out that I was one of the minority. I've always been curious about things. I pride myself on always being curious and exploring life. Why else be here? In this world, I mean. I believe if you always muster your curiosity then you'll ignite your life for the better. To not maintain your curiosity, I believe is to slowly and most certainly extinguish the flame in your soul. Die in instalments as Sadghuru says.

Look at me sounding all philosophical. Anyway...not here to preach. Let's get back on track. At first, after people grimaced at me for divulging my once hidden secret, I started to wonder if my pain threshold was just low, compared to most other people. Truth is, I still don't know. I do know after some research that pain is subjective, and can't truly be measured. There was a myth going around about impact on the scrotal sac being much more painful than giving birth. Which I'm sure would make any woman hearing that, want to kick a guy in the nuts. You know, just for research purposes.

Someone out there invented a unit for pain called 'Del'. You can do this nowadays, you see. With the advent of social media, anyone can put any bollocks out there and enough people read it, believe it and spread it, and before you know it — ignorance galore! So the claim was that giving birth was equivalent to 57 del units of pain, which was apparently similar to 20 bones getting fractured at the same time. A man being hit in the balls, was like having 200 bones fractured at the same time. Hopefully, anyone reading this can see that this is already sounding ridiculous. The unit may have come from the Latin word dol, short for dolor, which stands for sorrow or pain. It turns out, like I've already said, to be a load of bollocks. And yes I have purposely chosen the word bollocks. Lol. It would be criminal not to, I feel.

The balls are covered in pain nerves called nociceptors. Any sort of impact on your balls is painful, so that you're put off from hitting your balls, basically. Don't forget, the balls are essentially like ovaries hanging outside of a man. They are the 'family jewels,' as they call them, as they carry the substance for procreation. So, of course, nature wants to ensure the chances are not destroyed. When kicked in the balls, the pain also extends to the stomach via the vagus nerve. This induces vomiting; although I've never felt like puking when I've been kicked in the balls. Perhaps my nociceptors are wired differently. Who knows? Of course, when you puke, the plan is to turn you away from any more potential danger. You can't continue in a brawl if you're being sick. Your fighting opponent may also be disgusted and leave you be. Evolution and biology all have their reasons, you see. Even the appendix, which was thought to be a useless appendage on our intestine. It's now believed this acts as a reservoir for important gut bacteria, crucial for our immune system. Nothing is without purpose. We just may not know what the purpose is.

So there's been a lot of debate over which is the most painful. Giving birth or being kicked in the balls. And, as noted earlier, totally subjective. The one thing that is interesting is that one of them results in a possible baby, whilst the latter may result in someone never having a baby. A beautiful subtle paradox in life. Did I tell you I love paradoxes? Well, I do. Paradoxes and Ironies. I love spotting and sussing them out in life situations. Find it fascinating.

Of course, I was curious as to what got me into ballbusting. I needed to know why. Why me? Some people do it mainly to be humiliated and degraded. That is the turn on. They go to women to do it. And that is their thing. Where I'm different is I go to men to do it. Women hitting me in the balls just hasn't the same effect. I prefer men doing it. Sexually, I'm into women. I just have the added kink of enjoying men hitting me in the balls. I have no idea why or where it came from. Was it some porn I watched as a young lad that has ingrained in my memory? Who knows? All I know is, our brains are complex, and all sorts of wiring can happen in our neurone network. Some manifestations, not being good at all. Like paedophiles and serial murderers. The brain makes big, abstract and sometimes random connections, which leads to syntactic speech, creative intelligence or in my case, crazy arse kinks.

So the best I could get out of why I'm into the fetish CBT, is that it's a combination of having a liberal, educated and open upbringing. That has led to my openness and acceptance of ballbusting as a fetish. I can explore without personal judgement. Judgement from others is another kettle of fish. You know, I could say that one evening I went into a pub and I got into a fight and got kicked in the balls and bang...Had the best orgasm ever. But I'd be lying. There is frankly no major thing that got me into it. Unless I was abducted and instead of anal probing, was subjected to scrotum trauma in some alien ship, and then returned to Earth. That would probably make more sense.

Of course, I've been told of the risks. I could damage my sperm for good, if I'm not careful. I'm advised sometimes to freeze my sperm — you know, just in case in the future I wanted kids and had ruined my chances. That reminds me of this escort I visited once to kick me in the balls. I believe he had frozen his sperm, but for entirely different reasons, which I won't go into here. Let's just say I think it's disgusting. But everyone to their own. That's what makes us human. Our large complex brains and our random likes and dislikes.

Just as an anecdote to show how complex our brains are. There's this friend of mine who's gay. He used to always get aggressive in his relationships. When I queried this, his reply was that he found their habits annoying. He got aggressive each time and the relationship broke down. Eventually after four relationships — all leading the same way, I asked him to consider the problem was his. Of course he was at first taken aback by my bluntness. But he calmed down and decided to explore what I was getting at. I have great respect for people who reflect. It takes courage to look deep inside yourself and take responsibility.

I asked him to elaborate on what exactly his ex partners did that was so annoying. He said two of them chomped, slurped and smacked their lips when they ate. Another one used to hum incessantly and would always tap or click his pen. The last one snored really loudly when he slept. It was all to do with annoyance from sounds people made. Irrational responses, some would say. It turned out my friend had a rare mental disorder called Misophonia. A condition that causes panic or intense anger in people listening to specific noises. Evidently, it's linked to Obsessive-compulsive disorders. He sought CBT counselling to help him with this condition and is now in a loving relationship. Of course we both had a laugh over the double meaning of CBT. He's not completely cured, but at least he now knows what he has. After explaining to his present partner, they both navigate their relationship accordingly.

So, there you see. Our brains are weird. We're effectively at the mercy of our brains, in a way. However, our brains can be rewired. Proven. It just requires a lot of work on our part and a lot of repetition of new habits. Three weeks, allegedly, is the length of time it takes for the brain to rewire after repetition of a habit. I chose not to change my fetish. I enjoy it. So instead, I accepted it. I'm not hurting anyone other than myself...a little. Although once I did come close to looking into CBT to curb the habit.

I'm in a relationship with a bisexual woman. We have a healthy relationship and she accepts my kink. Yes...I told her. She is sometimes worried about me. About me hurting myself. But she's not bothered about me damaging my sperm as she's never wanted kids. So it works quite well. Sometimes, I even have the pleasure of watching or joining in with her and another woman. She goes for lipstick lesbians. That's what they call lesbians that aren't butch. Having sessions with my girlfriend and her hook-ups; now that's a real turn on. One I'm sure most heterosexual men will relate to. It's just a shame that some straight men feel that way about watching two women, but then have an issue with two men fucking. I've never seen the issue and personally think it's stupid and...well a double standard. But there you are. People will be people.

My girlfriend is fiercely independent. Amanda, she's called. She definitely rules the roost. If we were to ever have a roost. She's most certainly a wonderfully complex character. Switching on her gregarious side when in parties or entertaining and likewise embracing her introverted side when reading or making pottery or stained glass objects, which she absolutely loves. Mastering in Psychology and human relations, she works as a prison reformer.

She's often told me she feels most at home when she's in a prison. At first I never knew how to take this, but now I just leave her to it. She has the shiniest light brown shoulder length hair. She corrected me once about the time it takes hair to grow. Reputedly, it takes two to three years to grow from the forehead to the shoulders, based on calculations of hair growing an inch every month. Her eyes are dark brown and filled with mystery. When she's horny, they go lighter in colour. She never knew this. She has the most luscious lips. This she knows. She glosses them every chance she gets. She's the same height as me, so no one stands on tiptoes to steal a kiss. Her dress sense is conservative/casual and she compliments her colours effortlessly, always knowing which item of clothing will go with the other.

We both understand one another and I'd like to say she totally gets me. We always allow each other space. We seem to have a sixth sense when we've spent too much time together. Then we escape into our own thing, Amanda most likely turning to her stained glass activity and me to my ballbusting activity. What can I say, we allow each other to be and that's why I love her. That and the fact she is prejudice free and accepting. She has to, to be with a guy like me. I know that. I haven't mentioned that I love her. I'm not ready to. I think I loved her the very first week of dating. Her acceptance of my ballbusting interest was not the major deciding factor, but it was most certainly the icing on the cake!

There was once I got kicked in the balls a bit too hard; although I had asked that the guy not hold back. Completely my fault. I had communicated via text on a gay app, informing the escort of what I wanted and negotiating the price. The frozen cum escort, I called him. When I got there, he was a lot more good-looking than I'd envisioned. Sometimes, you can't tell from pictures. It was important that the guy was masculine. Otherwise I might as well have a girl kick me and, like I've already mentioned, that did nothing for me. So this guy took his leg back all the way and drove his foot into me hard and at the right angle. He made full contact. I had worn loose boxers so my testicles hung loose in my trousers. I instantly doubled up and collapsed. The pain was intense but made me cum instantly too. I orgasmed right there on the guy's floor and he just watched. When I eventually opened my eyes, I could see the concern expressed on his face. I put my thumb up to relieve his worry. It's all I could do. I couldn't speak. I was still swallowing my pain.

My girlfriend ended up taking me to A and E that evening. Embarrassing, to say the least. It took ages to come up with a story to tell the doctor. In the end, I said I'd slipped and fell at an awkward angle, hitting my crotch on an upturned stool. I studied the doctor's face to see if he believed the story. I didn't detect anything to tell me otherwise. Had to have an ice pack on my cullions for a few days, and my little man was out of action for a while too. My girlfriend was not best pleased. But she had ladies she could hook up with and she did that. I couldn't even watch, as that caused me pain. A complete bummer. I seriously reconsidered the ballbusting activity after that incident. But only for a few months. Then I was back into it, albeit with more caution to my limits.

Whilst having a break from ballbusting though, I decided to research more on sexual kinks and where they were derived from. I was particularly interested in antidepressants and their negative effects on sex drive. Everything I've read seems to correlate antidepressants with sex drive and the advent of some form of kink. As far as I could see though, no cause for a fetish has been conclusively established. Apart from that, it is often developed in puberty with a conditioning associated with masturbation. Some say it is developed in an individual with deep entrenched feelings of inadequacy. The fetish gives the person some sense of control.

They found that Selective Serotonin Reuptake Inhibitors (SSRI), (used to lessen the effect of Parkinson's disease), can also be used to curb and even stop certain sexual practices by decreasing the libido. However, often at a price. That being another out of the ordinary outlet being formed. An aberrant sexual desire. A fetish of some form. It's the same with antidepressants. I've always thought it's weird how the antidepressants or dopamine and serotonin affecting drugs mess with libido in these strange ways. Showing, in my opinion, that it's all to do with our brain chemistry.

I believe there needs to be more research around this. But of course that's dependent on people coming forward with their varied fetishes and sexual practises, and that is just something people are not willing to divulge. I don't necessarily think it's all to do with shame. Perhaps putting it all out there takes away the thrill and excitement too. And that would be defeating the objective. Besides, if people were to ever take it on, really explore the fetishes out there. They will have some work on their hands, cause I tell you, there are plenty and new ones keep coming up.

No, I'm not trying to take away the attention from my ballbusting activity. I'm just letting you know that there are possibly hundreds of different fetishes out there and there will always be new ones in the making. Why? Because our brains are extremely complex and there will always be new realms of neuron connectivity to explore in the mind. I liken it to the universe. As expansive as the universe is. So, the mind is vast. I believe we haven't even begun to touch the surface of our mind's potential.

Went off on a tangent there. Let's bring us swiftly back to my balls and my fascination with them, eh? Lol. I don't really know what else to say, to be honest. I seem to have veered off the subject every chance I had. Not sure I've done that deliberately. I don't have anything to hide about it. I just have nothing of relevance to say. I enjoy being kicked in the balls. Sometimes there is no rationale to what we do. Sometimes things just are as they are. I enjoy the intense pain. I have to say it is often the lead up to the actual event that is a turn on. The anticipation. That is the thing that's exciting. Same as the thrill of the chase. Some men, if not most, will relate to this. The anticipation of what to expect. Once that is achieved, the thrill is gone. The excitement has been dampened, so to speak.

Some people do not appreciate that you create other excitement with the person you're in a relationship with. Instead they chase the next person — have an affair — to get the missing excitement. It's all just a game really. Some get lost in it and just want to continue playing the game, not realising that in a sense, the excitement of the anticipation is somewhat of an illusion. If you get lost in that loop, there is no climax. There is no end to get to. It takes perhaps a lot of experience and a lot of hookups to eventually see that the climax they are looking for, the continuous thrill, cannot be sustained. Wiser men, I guess you could say, realise this in good time, and learn to make peace and accept the melancholy of relationships. They learn to find joy and excitement in the simpler things. But we're not all the same. Some men, like me, need that constant thrill. It's the only thing that keeps us grounded in a sense. To get our fix and be with it. I am so, so lucky to be with a woman that understands this. I can enjoy the thrill from two aspects. I do know how lucky I am and I'm extremely grateful.

I understand how some of you reading this may be disappointed. There is hardly any explanation for my kink. I get that. But, you know what, I have come to accept that sometimes in life there is no meaning to stuff. Some things just are and we have to learn to just roll with it. Here I am, a partnered straight guy, who on the side likes getting kicked in the balls by men. It is what it is. That's what I like. End of.

AEA

Hey guys! Dean here! I've been reading this blog for some time now and have to say, I've been very impressed with the openness and blunt honesty. Very impressed indeed. I have something to share that I dread sharing with people in my life. I feel like I can do it here — actually I feel like I will be doing a service, because it's quite a dangerous practice. But I feel it's one that...if people were just more open about it and didn't feel obliged to do it in dark rooms on their own, could be avoided. The dangerous element to it, I mean. Anyway, before informing you of this fetish of mine, I should tell you a little about myself. That seems to be the social etiquette from what I can see...right?

I'm 5 feet, 10 inches tall. I have mousy brown hair and blue eyes. Not quite sky blue, more like ocean blue. Deep ocean blue. I'd say I'm quite a deep person. I guess my eyes mirror that. They change colour too, especially when having a go with my fetish. The colour change can be quite dramatic, I've been told by people experimenting with me. I have an athletic body. I enjoy playing squash and recently joined a team. Partly so as to curb my fetish a bit, as it was getting a bit much. Too much of a good thing is not good for you, apparently. Lol. I also enjoy going to the gym and swimming, and more recently I joined a martial arts class. Learning Taekwondo and really loving it.

I recently turned 30 and I've been very lucky in life so far, I'd say. I have a job I enjoy. Work for a housing association and it's a fantastic company. I wouldn't say I'm a climber though, I haven't really been bothered about climbing the career ladder, so to speak. It's more important to me to be happy. I don't like unnecessary stress. I guess there's a slim line between stretching yourself so as to grow and being stressed to the point of being unhappy. I just want to be happy. But I do have to take a reflective look now and again to make sure I'm not being too safe either. We function best when we have some dose of certainty but also a dollop of uncertainty too. Both are required for us humans reputedly, so there you go.

So here goes... the cookie crumbling moment. My secret pastime is... Autoerotic asphyxiation, AEA for short. Some of you would have heard about it on the news. Mostly when it has gone wrong and someone has accidentally killed themselves. A famous actor known for the movie Kung Fu, but even more so for Kill Bill, killed himself this way. David Carradine. Just thought then — I recently joined a martial arts class. Weird!! Lol I'm not superstitious. Doesn't mean anything. But it's a dangerous act, my fetish I mean — one I'm fully aware of and so always put precautionary measures in place. You have to. But the other reason I decided to share this with you all is to reveal something else — I always thought I was the bachelor type. Not bothered about meeting someone. Quite happy just having fun. You know... of the sexual variety. Some part of me always thought that my desire to be strangled was too much for most and no one would be willing to get into a relationship with me having that as a fetish. And so I kind of resigned to the possibility of being on my own for good and being okay with that. Recently though, I met this guy and it changed everything.

I will tell you all about it. But let's explore where this breath control play of mine may have come from.

I've always had quite a high sex drive. More so than most I think. As soon as I have too much free time. I tend to want to get my kit off and play with my wiener. That's why I've endeavoured to put things in place to keep me busy. I know it's not all about sex. But God, I do love sex. Very much. ;)

I was the middle child of my parents. Have an older brother and a younger sister. None of my family knows about my fetish. And that's why... sorry didn't want to admit this, but my real name is not Dean. Just in case. I know. One day. I wish to be totally open. But I just don't want to worry my family. We're quite a close family. I'm closer to my mum than my dad, I'd say. Possibly a gay man's cliché, but there you are. I adore my mum. This likely causes some sibling rivalry between my older brother and me, being as older sons tend to be closest to their mums. But there is quite an age difference between me and my brother, so that probably helps.

It's hard for me to admit this. More so because a lot of mothers, parents, lost their teenage sons to this. I used to be into what was called the choking game from a very early age. I think around 10 or 11 years old. Not so much of a sexual thing then, but certainly about feeling high. When I was 12 it was the first time I found it sexually stimulating. I had returned home from school and went straight to my bedroom. For some reason I was feeling horny as hell that afternoon. It may have had something to do with me and four other lads wrestling in the playground. None of them knew I was gay. I wasn't sure I knew I was gay. I just remember loving wrestling. The sweaty bodies, the tight holds and grasps. One particular guy started to play-strangle me. I know it's dodgy to use the word 'play' straight before 'strangle', but there you go. Don't know how else to say it. The guy was strangling me but not with all his might, just messing about it. But it properly turned me on. I couldn't wait to get home to masturbate. That's probably the first time I realised I had a submissive side. I was horny as hell. I'm sure he was too. Because I'm sure as we were wrestling he had a hard on. I felt it as we tumbled on the lawn in the playground. Quite a big one too. The erection, not the lawn. That's what got me going.

As soon as I was in my room I stripped my clothes off. My parents wouldn't be back for another hour or so. I decided to hold my breath as I was having a wank. Wanted to see how long I could hold my breath for.

As a swimmer, I particularly enjoy underwater swimming. Probably for this same reason, although I hadn't thought about that before. Hmmmmmm. Interesting. Anyway, the more I held my breath and then let go just as I was struggling, the higher I got from it. Got proper giddy and lightheaded and this made the orgasm more extreme. I shot my load right over the bed, literally two to three feet away, and it hit my wardrobe door, making a satisfying thud sound as my spunk made impact. I had never come so much in my life. It was extreme for sure. I lay there panting, watching as my spunk dribbled down the wardrobe door.

That was pretty much the start of it for me. You don't forget something so significant as that when you're that age. Most young boys love sex. 'Filled with cum', as a friend of mine used to say, and 'desperate to off load.' And if some activity got more out of you then all the better. So I guess it was no surprise that I became fixated about it. In no time I started experimenting with strangulation. But I hasten to say I was shaken up real bad when I made myself unconscious once. I had tied a belt to my wardrobe door, yes — the same wardrobe door I had spunked on. Was watching porn whilst having a wank. The plan was that if I got carried away then the belt would eventually give, if it was getting too tight. I would drop and the belt would give and I would drop to the floor with my neck free. This one time, that didn't happen. I went unconscious and instead of the belt loosening, the belt bar got stuck in one of the holes and held me in position. Luckily, the drop was enough to crack my knee on a desk. That jolted me back into consciousness and I managed to reach up to loosen the belt. A very close call. It really shook me up and I have never used a belt after that. Yeah, I know what you're all probably thinking. Why would I even continue? What can I say? When you have a 'bug,' it's hard to shift it. I'm into it. It's like, a normal orgasm just doesn't do it for me. When you're into something, it's hard to change, especially where sex is involved.

I have this friend who is into being fisted, in a big way. Emphasis on the 'big.' He'd be strapped in a harness and get fisted by guys all queuing up to have a go. This one morning, on a Sunday, no less, when others would be getting ready to go to church. The guys were all high on drugs, one guy shoved his arm in, so fast and hard that it ruptured his colon. Literally split his intestine in half. He had to be rushed to hospital, operated on and was out of work for about 6 months. The guy who caused the damage was so remorseful. I think he stopped fisting people after that. Did my friend stop being fisted? Nope. As soon as he was healed, he got straight back into it. He just made sure people were not high on drugs. He believed if judgement wasn't tampered with, then all should be fine. So he carried on. For him, part of the turn on is being submissive too. Same as me. The dynamic of having someone dominate you to that extreme, unquestionably heightens the pleasure for us passive men. Something you just wouldn't understand, unless you were submissive.

Needless to say, I learned from my mates' experience. I made sure never to mix AEA with drugs or alcohol. No poppers either. I figured you need your senses in full check when messing around with your neck in that way. I'll always owe my friend for that. Totally indebted to him. He possibly saved my life, up to now anyway. I made sure he was around when I was in need of a strangulation orgasm. That way he could keep an eye out and ensure my safety. And he did a pretty good job too. He brought me around a couple of times. I could easily have zoned out and ended up running towards or away from a massive orb of light, depending on what your spiritual affiliation is. He was always understanding and never judging. A stalwart friend through and through. We grew very close. I put my life in his hands, in a way. That's the ultimate I would say, in creating a strong bond with someone. So it hopefully won't be surprising to you, the reader, that after about 2 years of intense friendship we decided to start dating. Well... we didn't do too much dating to be fair. We had been dating for two years. We desperately wanted to feel each other naked and we moved swiftly into that phase.

It's funny when you're friends with someone and you don't necessarily look at each other in a sexual way and then one day you do. He has the fittest body. A great arse! Definitely the best bubble butt I've ever seen. That certainly helped when I had to switch from being passive to playing the dominant role. He has the most amazing green eyes. Almost like polished malachite. Luscious lips. A stubble, and amazing hands. When he touched me - I swear it sent an electric current through me. Kissing him made me lose myself. We'd kiss for ages and it just happened naturally and before long I would be playing with his butt. Rimming him and fingering him. Eventually, a few weeks in, I eased a finger at a time into him. Eventually my cupped hand was in him and with some more lube and effort, my hand was in him up to my wrist. Whilst in him he instructed that I make a fist and then slowly pull my hand out.

Before doing this I had to psyche myself up. I knew what had happened to him. He had a large scar on his abdomen to prove it, which I occasionally kissed when we were making love. So, obviously I had some anxiety around it all. But, oh my god, when we did get into it, it was the most sensual thing I've ever experienced. The only sexual thing that took me to heightened orgasm without having to be strangled.

Occasionally, Brendan...that was his name, would grab my neck whilst he was riding me. Watching him bounce and grind his bubble butt on my cock was a turn on enough. But when I was about to come, he would grab my neck tightly with his hands. It baffled me how the both of us brought out the hidden dominant part of us. He knew the exact amount of pressure to use and exactly where to place his hands. You have to avoid putting pressure on the vagus nerve in your neck, you see. We didn't even have to put safety mechanisms in place. Like tapping three times gently or letting go of something you're holding in your hand, as a way of indicating you'd had enough. Brendan had watched me masturbate so many times. He knew exactly what to do. He was possibly the safest person I could enjoy my fetish with. And luckily we got together. There is someone for everyone, you see. It's true.

The day it happened for us was just the most magical, romantic time I've ever had. It was literally mind-blowing. And I should know about mind-blowing. I'd had enough dopamine, serotonin and endorphins rush into my brain from strangulation, to cause me the most intense head spinning exhilaration. So in order to beat that, it had to be downright spectacular, and it was.

I had just moved into my own flat. I had saved up enough for a deposit whilst living, or should I say scrounging, off my parents. Hard not to these days. Renting and buying now is next to impossible for young people on basic salaries. An ongoing housing crisis. I took some solace in knowing I was doing something about it in my role as a housing officer. Brendan had been a star in helping me move in. The flat was on the second floor of a very modern block of flats. It had a solar panel on the roof and even had a herb garden, a water feature, and lounge area for all the residents to enjoy. The only thing left to install was a swimming pool. Then we could lie on loungers and imagine we were in Miami or somewhere similar. The view from the rooftop was amazing. You could see all of the town of Windermere, which is where we lived, as well as all the hills in the distance. You could also see the Windermere lake, (largest in England), and the castle from the rooftop too. I think the town has a population of about 10,000, I reckon, without checking on Google. I knew I was very lucky to be living there. Very lucky indeed.

We had just unpacked everything and we were knackered. Completely pooped, as my nan used to say. We both decided to get a takeaway. And we wanted it greasy. So we ordered fish and chips, and we chilled and ate it in the living room. The living room needed some work doing to it. We had some white wine. Both of us enjoyed that.

You know what...I can't keep this up. You may have noticed a change in tense or writing style. That's because we don't live there anymore. I'm Brendan writing this now. I wanted to continue as Dean for much, much longer. But it's just too hard. You see Dean passed away suddenly.

He had started this blog and wanted it to go on this forum. He thought the forum had a very important purpose. To normalise the perceived abnormal and take away the taboo and shame associated with it. He believed that putting it out there could save lives. It was only right that I continued this. Tried my best to finalise it and put it out there, which is what I'm doing. I'll come back to it tomorrow though. I need some time...

Sorry about that...just needed some time. Still grieving you see. It's very hard, but I have wonderful memories. Dean was an exceptional human being. Don't get me wrong, he was also a pain in the arse...literally. Lol. We used to jest about eulogies and how they always painted the deceased in the best light and how funny *and* refreshing it would be to hear a negative tribute instead. Even if as a joke. For example, "He was a loving husband but a complete bastard as a friend." or "Most amazing sister one could ever have, but God she never shut the fuck up." We both had a very dark sense of humour and that's one of the things that bonded us.... I'm trying my best to lighten the tone here. Probably not doing the best job, but hey ho. Dean was the writer, not me. I do, however, have to do my best to narrate what he saw as an amazing tie between us. What he perceived as magical and which I am pleased he viewed that way, cause I felt exactly the same way.

We had just moved in. We ordered fish and chips from our local — Happened to be one of the best in town. We were both healthy eaters normally, but we made exceptions now and again. And we enjoyed it. We always did something extra, in the form of exercise, to make up for it the next day. We opened the window as it was quite muggy. We needed a storm and some rain. We sat down on the floor, next to a side table, like the Japanese would do. And we ate in silence whilst looking at each other. Something happened that evening that I'll always remember. As we were eating our fish, two common blue butterflies flew in through the open window. They could have been chalk hill blues which are a rare species. That would have made this even more spectacular. But I couldn't be sure. They fluttered around as if engaged in an air dance. One fluttered around Dean and the other fluttered around me, and then they danced in the air together, before our eyes. It was the most beautiful thing. It was like they were swimming in the air. Scientists have marvelled over how butterflies do this. They discovered that they combine at least four different aerodynamic mechanisms in order to achieve this majestic dance in the air. We, as humans, are yet unable to replicate this with technology.

Now, this could very well have been a coincidence. I get that. But you know what takes this to another level. Dean loved the book "Hope for the flowers." It was one of his best books, and it was about butterflies. I read it and loved it instantly. Such a simple, yet very poignant book about the human condition. These two butterflies danced around us as we sat gawking, with half filled mouths. Dean was right. It was magical. We both looked at each other and we both knew what each other were thinking. We knew it was a sign. It would be our little universal magical secret. We moved in closer and we kissed. I swear it was like the universe imploded on itself. The electricity was intense to say the least. After some time… although time didn't seem to be part of our universe anymore; both of us opened our eyes together to witness both butterflies make one more fluttering dance around our heads and then fly back out the window. Needless to say, the sex we had that evening was pure Kama Sutra!

Before Dean, I had been in relationships where we stopped listening to one another. Relationships that were so damaging, now that I look back. Playing on our insecurities. I'm not sure people even know they're doing it, when in relationships. The power-play thing that people eventually fall into, by default. Before you know it, resentments take hold, because no one is really listening and the relationship inevitably becomes toxic. I remember being so scared of breaking up that I would bend over backwards to please the guy I was with. Lol. Yeah, I get it. You have your laugh. ;). I would turn into this submissive, pathetic, grovelling, pleasing shell of myself. Then he would appear to love me. He was controlling the shots you see. In order for him to be comfortable with *us,* he needed me to be weak.

Looking back now, it's clear he didn't love me, he just loved that I loved him so much. Of course, I had my part to play in this unhealthy dynamic. How fucked up is that? That was my experience of relationships for a long time and so I'd decided to stay single. Enjoying sex when I got it and losing myself in new hobbies and friendships. I made a point of seeing that there are numerous ways to bring joy into your life. It isn't just by falling in love with someone. You can fall in love with yourself, with nature. And I have to say, I was happy. I was actually content.

But then I got entangled with Dean, and it did take happiness to another level. There's always another level to happiness. Just like there's always another level to sadness, I'm sure. Dean listened to me with so much love. He listened in a way that made me feel I was the only one present in the Universe. There was no power play. We were equal. We nurtured each other's insecurities sensitively. Probably because we both didn't have that many. We had dealt with them ourselves whilst being single, and mastered and grown from them. Our understanding of each other was maintained. It was maintained, I think, because we also had our thing that we did for ourselves. We appreciated and respected our time apart and encouraged it when we could. We knew what we had was very powerful, and that made it even more likely, that we would want to hold onto it for fear of losing it. That's part of the human condition, you see. But that dynamic is no place for love to reside. We knew this innately. I'm not sure we ever talked about it. But I can say unequivocally, that we knew. We knew that in order for our love to be sustained, we had to resist holding on to it and just let it flow, and that's what we did. We had the most amazing three years living in that apartment in Windermere. We got engaged and were planning our marriage. That's when it happened.

It's a funny thing, because there was always that risk we were both privy to when satisfying his fetish. We both understood that. We had always been very careful. Him when fisting me and me when choking him before climax. I do remember the first time I choked him whilst riding him. His eyes must have changed into three or four shades of blue as oxygen stopped feeding his brain. They always went from light shades to darker shades as we progressed. It was quite fascinating to watch. We had tried other versions of cutting off the oxygen supply, like bag over head and smothering him with my arsehole, but strangulation was both our favourite, because we could look at each other and own what we were doing. I know that probably sounds crazy, but there you are.

It happened one muggy evening. He had returned from work early on a Friday, and he suggested we get fish and chips from our local. I was going to be a bit late from work. I worked in the local council as a planner. So both of us were into the housing sector. Doing our bit for the housing crisis. He was walking back with our fish and chips, and he had a heart attack and fell down dead on the street.

I'd like to think that it was sudden and quick and he didn't have any pain. More so I always wonder, as you'd imagine I'm sure, whether the cardiac arrest had anything to do with our sexual kink. But that's what he wanted. It made him happy to taste death whilst climaxing. They say to have an orgasm is like dying anyway, just a little. I guess Dean wanted to experience that a little bit more. Or course, the ego part of me could resent him and curse him for ever being into Autoerotic asphyxia. For ever continuing to take that risk, and now leaving me all alone. But that would only be my ego part talking. Look back at that victimising sentence. 'For ever', 'All alone' Boohoohoo.

Dean wanted to experience something in a more profound way. At the end of the day we're all here to experience. Dean had to die for me to truly get it. It's all interlinked somehow. Birth, orgasm and death. Dean enjoyed the connection between death and orgasm. He got it, probably more than any of us did. And now he rests after achieving the final and ultimate orgasm. I will always think of him fondly and I'll continue to live as powerfully as I can, experiencing as much as I can, as I know that is what he'll want. For those days when I'm feeling blue or just downright depressed, I will always remember that evening with the butterflies with a smile.

P.S. Dean's real name was Joshua by the way. I'm sure he won't mind me divulging that now. He's dead.

THE END

I plan on getting out volume two as quickly as my audience encourages me to ;)

Sexual Diary ;)

---

---

---

---

---

---

---

---

---

---

---

---

---

---

---

---

---

---

---

---

---

---

---

---

---

---

---

---

---

---

Printed in Great Britain
by Amazon

59461168R00080